SAR
powderhounds

Heather Kellerhals-Stewart

James Lorimer & Company Ltd., Publishers
Toronto

James Lorimer & Company Ltd., Publishers acknowledges the support of the Ontario
Arts Council. We acknowledge the financial support of the Government of Canada
through the Canada Book Fund for our publishing activities. We acknowledge the support of the Canada Council for the Arts which last year invested $24.3 million in writ-
ing and publishing throughout Canada. We acknowledge the Government of Ontario
through the Ontario Media Development Corporation's Ontario Book Initiative.

Cover design: Tyler Cleroux
Cover image: iStock

Library and Archives Canada Cataloguing in Publication

Kellerhals-Stewart, Heather, 1937-, author
        SAR powderhounds / Heather Kellerhals-Stewart.

Issued in print and electronic formats.
ISBN 978-1-4594-0518-9 (bound).--ISBN 978-1-4594-0519-6 (pbk.).--
ISBN 978-1-4594-0520-2 (epub)

        I. Title.

PS8571.E447S27 2013   jC813'.54   C2013-904177-X
C2013-904178-8

James Lorimer & Company Ltd.,   Distributed in the United States by:
Publishers   Orca Book Publishers
317 Adelaide Street West, Suite 1002   P.O. Box 468
Toronto, ON, Canada   Custer, WA, USA
M5V 1P9   98240-0468
www.lorimer.ca

Printed and bound in Canada.
Manufactured by Friesens Corporation in Altona, Manitoba, Canada in August 2013.
Job #87629

For Luka

contents

 *1 rope practice*

SATURDAY, 11:00 AM: CHIC

I'm in a dicey position here all right. And it's not surprising, if you know how my older brother operates. Josh has this habit of getting me into trouble, not that he really means to. But it's been this way forever. He's always been too smart for his own good. Mister Right, I call him. No matter how hard I try, I can't keep up with him.

"I'll let you go first on the highline we've rigged up, little bro. It'll be good practice," he said to me first thing this morning. And that's why I'm dangling from something like a zip line over a raging torrent, freezing my ass off. Not to mention my feet. I can already see the doctor, waving his scalpel and closing in on my toes. Sorry, your toes are too far gone. We'll have to amputate — all ten of 'em.

"How ya doing?" Josh shouts from the safety of the far bank.

"What?" I'm jolted out of my half comatose state.

"I said, how are you doing?"

"Knowing a bunch of you savvy search and rescue types are on my case, I'm doing just fine, thank you, except for my toes."

My brother ignores the sarcasm squeezing through my clenched teeth. Probably didn't even notice it because this is how we communicate when the going gets rough. Our old man is the same. It's quicker and easier than breaking out in a sweat.

"We'll have you across, matter of minutes," Josh says.

Oh, great. My brother Josh is an eternal optimist. No prob, it's foolproof, is his motto. For him, maybe. If you're standing beside him and lightning strikes, guaranteed you'll be the one to be hit.

I've only been hanging here for half an hour or so, thanks to a pulley that has somehow jammed. Trouble is, it might have been my fault. I watch the river surging below me. Lucky I'm going solo and not ferrying some badly injured person across this river. I swing my freezing feet below the mini-board on which my bum is sitting. Yeah, DOA — dead on arrival from hypothermia.

"Okay, we've got the other rope rigged up. No prob, just clip into it, Chic, and we'll have you across in a couple of seconds."

Guys are shouting orders back and forth from the cliffs above the river. A cold wind is starting to whine around my legs. I seem to be moving in slow motion. My dead fingers finally grab the spare carabiner on my harness and I clip myself onto the pull rope. Hope I've got it right. I keep my eyes focused on the guys ferrying me across. Better not to watch the water below, snapping at my feet. I can sure hear it, though.

Josh must be feeling guilty. I can hear him shouting over the roar of the river, "Don't worry, Chic, it's fool-proof." And this time he is right. No chance of me or anyone else screwing things up. Still, I'll be glad to be out of here. I feel the jerk on my body harness as the guys drag me up and onto the far bank.

Josh tilts my helmet back and peers into my face. "Sorry. I realize this was your first time practising rope rescue."

"Not your fault."

These glitches can happen to the best of outfits. It just had to be me dangling out there — the kid brother of the guy who heads our local volunteer search and rescue group. I've racked up plenty of time on other practice sessions — dry runs, everyone calls them, but I have never been on a real search and rescue mission. Why? I'm only seventeen, too young to be an official member of the crew. Josh keeps saying he'll take me along, maybe next time we get called out. I keep hoping.

Someone throws a blanket over my shoulders. A cup of hot chocolate is poured down my throat. A mustard-coated hot dog is staring me in the face. Maybe this was all planned. These guys just needed a victim. Me. Seriously though, they are true professionals, every one of them.

"Okay, let's get on with it," my brother says.

The crew jumps to attention, slurping down their cups of lukewarm coffee. We spend the rest of the afternoon fiddling with rescue pulleys and harnesses and ferrying people across the river. Successfully, I gotta say. Can't say as much for the weather. The sun has fizzled out behind clouds and by the time we decide to call it a day we're soaked through. It's a typical coast downpour and snowing higher up for sure. Definitely not a time to be running around in the mountains.

"Let's head for the pub; relax there and warm up," Josh says.

"You smell pretty rank. Doubt they'll let you in." Roc screws up his nose and pretends to back off. Though he's pushing forty and the oldest guy in the group, you'd never know it. He barely makes it to my shoulder but his sense of humour still flies.

More back and forth as Josh surveys the water-logged group. "Someone should stay in the office and keep an eye on our emergency line. It's Saturday, remember? The crazies may be out in the mountains."

I see nine heads swinging around and focusing on me. Can't drink legally, can't vote, can't be an official member of the group here, but I can sure stand guard in the office on a Saturday night. Party time for everyone but me.

"Okay, Josh, I can take the hint. But you'll keep your phone ready on the off chance a call comes through?"

"Don't be so sure there won't be a call, Chic. There will always be a few dim people running around in the mountains, even in abysmal weather. If you do hear anything we'll be back within minutes."

Clouds have obscured any view of the mountains. Probably whiteout conditions up there. It's hard to see past my arm with the rain pelting down. When we checked the weather report on the Web this morning it wasn't exactly promising — a series of storm systems moving in from the Pacific, with heavy rain at sea level and significant snowfall over the mountains. Yeah, I know it by heart.

2 powderhounds

SATURDAY, 1:30 PM: LUC

After a morning of hard skiing we're standing at the top of Outer Orbit, the steepest of the expert ski runs. Toru and Nick are on snowboards. Cass and I are sticking with skis, because we're training for our club's upcoming downhill races. Nick can't afford to hit the hills every weekend, even though he has an after-school job working at the fast food shack. He keeps rubbing it in how I have it so easy — rich parents and all that. But they don't take much interest in what I'm doing.

Toru's parents don't have a clue what skiing and boarding are all about. If they did he wouldn't be here today, they are that cautious. The four of us have different lives for sure, but we come together on the hills. And Cass can more than hold her own, as Nick keeps reminding me.

"What's holding you guys up?" Cass calls out.

Like all the extreme runs, Outer Orbit is marked with a double black diamond to warn off novice skiers. One look down should turn any beginner away. It's narrow, plus steep enough in some sections to get you airborne, which is half the fun.

"You boarders are sure wiping the slope bare with your clumsy boards," I say, giving Toru a friendly punch.

Toru just grins. He's used to my hassling him. And to parents who don't approve of "those young people or their activities" — a more-or-less accurate translation from their Japanese. Maybe a grin is his best weapon.

Nick jumps to his rescue. "Oh yeah? It's you skiers' fault." He does a fair imitation of a skier side-slipping down a slope and erasing all the snow.

"You sound like a bunch of politicians," Cass says. "Remember what we're all here for?"

"Right . . . skiing."

"No . . . boarding."

Cass swings her poles around and shoves off. "You're all hopeless. See you at the bottom."

"Wait at the junction with Bowling Alley," I shout.

"We can cut off the run there and carve some turns through the trees."

Then we're all heading down, whooping and yahoo-ing our way around moguls and slow skiers. I hit a rock uncovered by some dumb snowboarder and go cartwheeling down the slope behind the others. I get up, spit snow from my mouth and carry on. When I reach the junction the others are waiting for me.

"Ate some snow, eh?" Nick says with a grin.

I shrug. "So what are you waiting for, Nick?" I point to the fresh powder off the run.

There's a single ski track there, heading beyond the rope and sign that marks the edge of Outer Orbit and the patrolled area. Beyond that there's nothing but trees and powder snow and some great riding waiting for us. I check the sky and wind direction. Snow is definitely on the way. I'm a real weather freak. Sometimes if I go on and on about the weather Cass and the others tell me to shut up.

"Maybe heading out of bounds isn't such a great idea," Toru says.

"What? We agreed coming up on the chairlift that we'd go looking for some untracked powder."

"We did, but . . ."

"Then why go changing your mind, Toru?"

"I don't like looking for trouble, like some people do."

This isn't the first time that Toru has changed his mind at the last minute. We were skiing in the backcountry last winter and he wouldn't cross an easy slope because of possible avalanche danger.

"I guess you are thinking of that guy who skied out of bounds and got lost and was threatened with a fine," I say.

Toru nods. "Search and rescue had to call in a helicopter. It's a free service but if the skier had to pay it would have cost him a small fortune."

"But he wasn't mountain savvy like we are."

"Maybe . . . just don't think you can be right every time, Luc."

Cass skis past the sign and turns around to face us. "Is anyone else coming?" It's a good thing we have someone like Cass around to break up our endless arguments.

"Count me in," Nick shouts.

I see Toru looking around furtively. There's no ski patrol in sight. He touches the rope marking the ski area boundary like it's a sharp knife and slips past. I follow behind, almost trampling on his snowboard to make sure he doesn't turn back. We don't stop until we reach the shelter of the trees.

"Hope nobody saw us," Toru says.

"Quit worrying, Toru. Everybody knows this is where the powderhounds cut off the run."

Toru forces a grin. "I guess."

"Granola bar, anyone?" I pass around a few of the stale packages I always keep in my pack. No one's hungry except for a taste of the powder snow that's lying ahead of us. Cass leads the way again, and surprise — Toru lets loose with a wild whoop and takes off after her.

For once I'm happy to have a track ahead of us. I haven't been here since last year and this guy obviously knew what he was doing. The tracks are fresh. We follow them as they slice across the slope, heading down gradually.

"Right on," I yell to Toru who is ahead of me. We crisscross each other's tracks, playing tag around trees and tossing up snow clouds. My skis are floating in the deep powder — I'm as near to flying as I'll ever get.

"Whoa." Toru comes to a stop beside Cass. Then Nick and I come down to earth behind him, out of breath.

3 *out of bounds*

SATURDAY, 2:15 PM: LUC

We've reached the opening in the trees where you have to head straight down. Keep traversing and you'll find yourself caught in cliffs that encircle the mountain and then drop sheer into a lake. Suicide Scarp, the area is called, and it's maybe 400 metres from top to bottom. Hikers run into trouble here every summer.

"Well?" Cass turns to face the three of us.

The slope below us is steep and narrows into a gully near the bottom. We look for the skier ahead of us, but there are only his tracks there, carving up the slope.

Nick whistles. "Pretty impressive show for a guy on telemark skis."

"The slope looks stable enough and the snow isn't

showing any cracking or sloughing beneath my skis," Cass adds.

"Good to know, Cass, but I'd feel better if we had avalanche beacons along," Toru says.

"So . . . are we going after our skier or not?" I leave without waiting for Toru's or anyone else's answer.

I hear Cass poling behind me and Nick nudging his board into action. I keep my skis in the fall line. Turns are tight and becoming more cramped as the gully nears. Cass flies by and leaves me in a dust of snow. Though she doesn't say a word, I know she's smiling. There's no way I can catch her. Into the gully we go. Snow slides away beneath my skis and a moment of panic grips me, but the tongues of snow slither to a stop. And I'm on my way again.

"Aaah . . ." I barely make it across the hole where our telemark skier took a tumble. I silently swear at him as I wobble on one ski but manage to right myself. Then I take off after Cass again.

Behind me and almost catching up are the two boarders. They whoop and holler, thinking I'm out of the competition, but they're out of luck. The trees streak past, like poles beside a race track. I gulp down snow and air.

Cass is a speck way below me. She has found a good place to stop and is waiting there to see us all safely down.

Cass is careful. That's not surprising — she's just like her parents, who coach our racing team.

Seconds later the gully spills me into a clearing above the cross-country track where Cass is standing. I schuss towards her and do a hockey turn, spraying her with snow. I'm so pumped with adrenaline after the powder run that I half forget we're just ski buddies and I give her a humungous bear hug.

"Sweet," she murmurs.

"Really?"

"I mean the run."

"Oh . . ."

Within seconds Nick is standing beside us, too stunned after the run to let loose with his usual talk. "Where's Toru?" I ask him.

"Not sure. I heard him shout. It sounded like he needed to adjust something on his board. It wasn't a good place to stop, so I just carried on. He'll be fine."

"We'd better wait for Toru," Cass says.

I check my watch. Almost three o'clock. We have to keep moving if we want one last run before the lift closes.

As usual Cass has a pretty good idea of what I'm thinking. "You and Nick go on. I'll wait for Toru. And if we don't make it in time, you two head up the hill."

"Yeah, we better keep our friend Luc happy — he's

that focused on one last run. If there's time, we might grab something to eat as we go past the lodge."

"There won't be time, not if we want to catch the last ride up, Nick."

I glance up the hill. No sign of Toru yet. Nick has his snowboard under one arm and is already walking up the cross-country run. I unfasten my skis, sling them over my shoulder and head after him. But I feel a twinge of guilt when I see Cass waiting back there.

The lodge is crammed with skiers packing up for the day. Fair-weather types, I call them. Nick detours to pick up some fries, while I keep a lookout for the others. "Make it quick," I tell him.

When he arrives back he is carrying the fries, plus two giant-size coffee containers. He hands me one. "I don't like coffee, Nick."

"It isn't coffee."

I take off the top and look inside. Beer! "You know I don't drink the stuff, Nick. And you're not supposed to take beer outside the lodge."

He slaps me on the shoulder. "I know. Why do you think I poured it into coffee cups? Drink up, kid. It'll keep you warm on the hill."

I know, and Nick knows, that alcohol does not keep you warm. He's a year older than the rest of us and always manages to buy beer for everyone. I don't want to waste time arguing, so I start gulping the stuff down. I should have eaten something, but Nick has polished off all the food. I shove some money at him. "I'm heading out to the lift."

"Ree-lax, kid, it's not the end of the world if we miss the last run."

Outside the wind is picking up and the sky has turned a suspicious grey. I join the few people milling around the lift entrance. Nick follows, balancing his snowboard under one arm and waving toward the cross-country run with the other. "Hold on, Luc. I see them coming."

 4 into the outback

SATURDAY, 3:15 PM: LUC

"Last ride up," the lift attendant warns us.

Cass poles herself onto the ramp beside me, just in time. She does it smoothly, same as when I'm sitting beside her at school and she's breezing through a tough math question. Toru and Nick are doing their usual snowboard shuffle. I call it the kangaroo hop because boards are hopeless on flat ground. The lift attendant shouts at us to keep moving.

I grin back at his sour face. "Maybe we'll squeeze in another run after this one," I call to him.

"Just try it." He waves us forward as the empty chair rolls around. With a desperate leap the two boarders make it and together we wait to get airborne. "Nothing like cutting it close," Nick says. He swings his board around and damages my shin.

"Careful, will you?"

We lean back and feel the lift accelerating. It's fun to watch the kids yelling and bombing down the beginner run below us. Soon the noise is left behind and there is only the silence of snow-draped trees. This is my world — the mountain world, away from the pressures of home and school. I'm happy alone, but having Cass alongside me is a real bonus. I curl one arm around her shoulder to keep us warm.

Toru lifts the safety bar as we near the top station. "Visibility is getting worse," he says, flicking a stray snowflake from his jacket.

The four of us slide off the lift and stand there aimlessly for a moment, wondering where to go next. "What'll it be for our last run?" I ask finally.

The guy sitting snug and warm in the lift shack yells at us to keep moving.

"Relax, there's nobody behind us," Nick tells him.

"I'm heading down Powder Hound — it's the shortest way back to the lodge. Given the weather that seems the smart thing to do," Toru says.

"Yeah, directissima," Nick chimes in. "Those fries I ate are crying for company."

"I'm with you," Cass says. "I'm cold after sitting on the lift."

"I dunno . . . I'm thinking one last powder run. Visibility should be fine in the trees," I say.

"Getting late."

"Tired."

"Looking like whiteout conditions."

"Food sounds good."

"So Powder Hound it is, agreed?"

I listen to the usual excuses. It sounds as if the crew has made up its mind. "Meet you at the bottom then. I'll take Outer Orbit and if visibility looks half decent I'll detour through the trees again."

I'm about to pole off when Toru grabs my shoulder. "Listen Luc, it's the end of the day and we're all tired. We should stick together."

With all that powder snow waiting for me I don't need another Toru lecture. I shake his hand off my shoulder. "I'll see you all at the bottom."

"Toru is right, we should stay together," Cass says.

"Look, it's no big deal. It's not as if I'm planning a solo march to the South Pole."

Toru shrugs and turns away. "We'll wait for you at the downhill lodge, then."

"And order some food for you if the cafeteria starts

shutting down," Nick adds.

"Sure, sure, do whatever you want. You won't have to wait long for me, guaranteed."

"You can't go alone," Cass says in her no-nonsense tone. She doesn't use it that often, only when she is dead serious.

Toru nods his head and smiles at her. Even Nick joins in without any mention of food this time. What is this, a conspiracy? I pole off in a spray of snow, not waiting for more talk. A minute later Cass bombs past me and we turn together into Outer Orbit. No surprise that she is following me. We stop where we did before. Wind has blown snow into our tracks and only a few marks are visible. Far below us, I see a single skier, awkwardly fighting his way down.

I turn toward Cass, searching for something, anything, to say. "A quick run through the powder and Nick won't even have time to think about food. Right?"

A long moment of silence, except for the whumph as a branch unloads snow. I brush the snow off my face and let it melt in my mouth. My mouth feels dry after drinking that beer Nick gave me. I could get the water bottle out of my pack, but we'll be down at the bottom in half an hour if we push it. So why bother?

"What do you say, Cass?" She has stalled me with

a look that scans my face for god-knows-what. It goes through me and exits the other side. And it doesn't feel great. "Well?"

"I think we should stay on the run. It looks too murky in the trees."

"Murky — that's a weird word. Look, you don't need to come. I'm fine on my own. Head down the run and tell the others I'm coming."

"I'm not leaving you on your own. End of discussion, okay?"

I give up. We're about to head off when the ski patrol, doing a final sweep of the run, swoops down on us. "You two all right?"

"We're fine. But I'm not so sure about him." I point to the skier below us who is still struggling — side-slipping and scraping the snow down to bare ice.

The ski patrol shakes his head. "I better head down and help him out of his misery or he'll be here all night." He pushes off, executes a jump turn, then slides backward facing us. "You're following me, right? I need to know that everyone is off the hill."

"Yes, we're just taking a breather."

"Good."

He swivels into another jump turn and speeds downhill. Uh-oh, I can sense trouble coming with Cass.

"We should follow him down, Luc. We said we would. If he discovers we've gone out of bounds we're in major trouble. I know what my parents would say."

"There's no way he can find out. You think he'll be lying in wait for us down below?"

Before Cass can toss out more arguments I ski past the rope that marks the edge of the patrolled area. I don't look back because I know she will follow.

Although snow has drifted into our ski tracks, I can still make out the puncture marks made by our poles. Once we're in the shelter of trees, I can actually see tracks here and there. But as Cass said, it is sort of murky with the trees overhead, blotting out the sky.

I stop and wait for Cass, who has fallen behind. "The snow is great, eh?"

"Are you still following tracks?"

"More or less. But even without tracks I know the way."

"Things look different when it's snowing, Luc."

I don't bother answering her. If we keep traversing the slope and heading down, we'll be fine. The only sound is the swish of our skis and now and again the whip of tree branches against our jackets. Snow sifts silently into the tracks we leave behind. Even the usual squeak of my ski binding has been muffled by the weight of the snow.

The effort of cranking turns around trees has got me sweating. I stop, pull the water bottle from my pack and hand it to Cass. She swallows a few mouthfuls and then hands it back. "There's not much left."

"I didn't fill the bottle. Why carry extra weight around? It's not as if we're skiing in the backcountry."

"With all this snow falling it sure feels like backcountry."

"Look, Cass, we're only a few minutes off a groomed run in a big ski resort. Backcountry it's not."

But Cass's mood is rubbing off on me. I suddenly notice there are no ski tracks or pole marks ahead of us. All I can see are tree trunks plastered with snow and more snow falling and falling. If we were above tree line this would be a serious whiteout. I was caught in one once and it made me feel dizzy, almost sick. And right now I'm not feeling that great.

"But people do get lost. Look at that couple who got lost for days outside a ski run. One of them actually died of hypothermia."

"Cass, I know where we are. I wish you'd be more upbeat. We need to keep moving and get down — fast. I don't want Toru doing something dumb like notifying the ski patrol."

I'm still checking for tracks. We have to hit the

opening dead on or we're in trouble. Go too high and we'll overshoot it and get caught on Suicide Scarp. Too low and the bush and rocks make it impossible to move.

Cass grabs my arm to make sure I'm listening. "I don't know the country like you do, Luc, but I have the feeling we've stayed too high. I think we should try to backtrack."

"Trust me, Cass, it'd be way too difficult backtracking in this deep snow. Besides, I'm sure the opening is just ahead."

What I omit saying is this: I don't like the scenery and I don't like our timing and I don't like the fact that we're not following any tracks. I put my water bottle away, do up my pack and we're off again. It'd be nice if we could see some sky. The trees are shutting us in. Snow is covering my jacket and everything else. And now the unspoken question hangs between us: Where exactly are we?

5 lost

SATURDAY, 4:35 PM: LUC

Cass grabs my arm and stops me. "You keep talking to yourself, Luc. Are you all right?"

"How about you?"

"Tired."

I shake the snow off my skis and take off my pack. I hand Cass a half granola bar. It's the last of my food, except for a half-eaten apple left over from lunch.

"What about you, Luc?"

"I'm not hungry," I lie. Even a plate of Nick's greasy fries would go down well, might ease my headache. I take a swig of water from my bottle instead. "I don't get it. We should have reached the opening by now."

"You think we've stayed too high and missed our opening?"

"I don't know."

I can't say the L-word, not yet. But fear grips me, like it did that time a year ago when I was climbing solo. I'm back there again — clinging onto the rock face 40 metres above ground. I can't move. There's no rope and nobody to help me.

"Luc, we have to move. My fingers are freezing."

"Sorry, Cass, I'll get us on track again."

"Sorry? We don't have time to be sorry. It'll be dark soon."

"I know, I know. Give me half a minute to figure this out."

What to do . . . I haven't brought along any of my usual backcountry equipment, like a GPS that would've tracked our course. I do have a phone. I try it. Like I thought — there's no coverage this far around the mountain. The wind is picking up, and my thoughts spin with the snow coming down. No sounds from the ski area can reach us here . . . the runs are closed down . . . smart people will be inside.

With snow covering her jacket and ski pants, Cass has become a ghost like the trees around us. But her voice sure comes loud and clear.

"We don't have a map, we don't have a GPS, we don't have cell phone coverage, we don't even have a compass. It's looking like guesswork, if you ask me."

"You forget I know the terrain here."

"In good weather, maybe."

I unzip my pack and hand Cass some extra gloves I brought along. "They're dry. You can warm your hands, at least."

"Thanks, Luc. Sorry for sounding so negative."

"I don't blame you for being angry, Cass. But, like I said, I'll figure a way out of this mess."

"Uh-huh. You or somebody else?"

"How about that ski-patrol type we met? Guaranteed he'd leap from his helicopter, rescue you, and decide to leave me behind."

We stare at each other and start laughing — two crazies knee-deep in snow. I brush the snow off Cass's hood. "Look, here's my plan. We carry on for another ten minutes to make sure we've gone far enough. Then, if we don't find the opening, we turn and head back to the ski hill."

"With our downhill skis and boots it would be almost impossible to head back up. You said so yourself, Luc, remember?"

"I know we can't follow a steep uphill track, but if we

head gradually down we should hit either the opening or the ski hill."

"Let's hope you're right, Luc. I bet the others are worrying."

With Cass's words trailing after me, I pole off. What if we don't find the opening or the ski hill? I spent a night on Suicide Scarp last summer after I wandered off the trail looking for a shortcut. It was no picnic finding my way through the maze of cliffs and ledges. And that was summer.

I'm so wound up in my own thoughts I hardly notice the scenery going by. I hear Cass talking. "Luc, I think we should turn."

I manage to drop my mitts while I'm looking at my watch. Now there's snow inside them. I shake them out. "You're right, Cass. We've been going for over ten minutes. We have to turn."

She pulls up beside me. We stare ahead, not talking. What's left to say? We can't see anything except trees crowding each other out — smaller now, because the slope is steeper. Just a whole bunch of little sticks poking from the snow like hair on someone's head.

I hear Cass taking a deep breath. "I'll start off breaking trail, okay?"

"No way. I got us in this mess, so I'll do the trail breaking."

"Then say when you want me to take over."

I do a kick turn and plough past Cass. For a few minutes it's possible to follow our old tracks, until the angle becomes too steep. I watch the tracks above us disappearing and leaving us on our own. "That's it," I mumble.

"What?"

"Nothing."

I try to keep my skis on a level course, but I keep slipping. I can't get any traction in the powder snow. To propel myself forward I have to punch my poles into the snow, hard. The snow is so deep I have to keep increasing the downhill angle of my skis, or I stall. To make things worse, the wind is no longer behind us. Snow barrels into my face and stings my eyes. I bend my head, trying to shield my eyes, and it finds a way down my neck.

Cass is struggling behind me.

"Uh . . . watch out, Cass."

I lose traction, slip backwards, and find myself running over her skis. I knock her off balance and we both go over. The more we struggle, the deeper we dig ourselves into the snow.

"Cass, try and place your skis sideways, beside mine."

With both my poles resting on her skis I shoulder myself up. I almost make it, and then my poles skid off

and down I go again. Next time I wedge them behind
Cass's boots and push down until my arm muscles are
screaming. It works — I'm up. But Cass is still drowning
in snow.

"Take off your gloves, Cass, so I can get a better grip
on your hand." With me pulling, she finally staggers onto
her feet. I bend over my skis, exhausted with the effort.

Cass wipes the snow off my shoulders. "Looks like
the icing on some fancy cake."

She's trying to keep it light and not blame me. The
thing is, I'm not used to finding myself in trouble like
this. I know the mountains. I don't take stupid risks. I'm
used to looking after myself, because my parents sure
don't bother. I take a moment to silently rehash where
I went wrong. To tell the truth I'm not sure of anything
now. And it doesn't help that I'm thirsty and hungry.

"Are you okay?" Cass peers into my face.

"I'm wondering whether it's safe to keep heading
down. Not that there's much choice. We need to move
while there's still light."

"Let me break trail for a while."

"No, I'll go."

I point my skis downhill, just enough to keep
moving without much poling. I'm cruising along and
the thought of food and the lodge is beginning to look

real, when I notice a change. Not in the weather — it's still snowing — but in the light coming from above. Everywhere there are openings in the trees. The slope is steeper too. This could mean rock under the snow, maybe cliffs.

I feel Cass tapping my shoulder with her pole. "Careful. It looks really steep up ahead."

"I'll go easy, don't worry."

What do I know? Maybe we should stop. Then where do we go? It's looking more and more like a jigsaw puzzle and I have to find the right pieces. The opening ahead looks negotiable. Cass is following close behind me. I hear a steady stream of *Go slow, Be careful* . . . But the fact is we have to keep moving.

I'm onto the opening. It's steeper than I thought — 35 degrees is a guess. I can't see clearly, but it looks as if the slope ends in a cliff. I edge my skis into the snow, trying to stomp out a track for Cass. Suddenly snow slides away beneath my skis and slips over the cliff below me. A puff of snow hangs in the air as if to mark the spot. With a frantic poling effort I propel myself across the remaining slope and grab onto a small tree.

"Stay where you are," I shout back to Cass.

Too late. She has already started across. When she hits the spot where the snow slid, her added weight brings more from above and she's knocked off her feet. All I can see is a jumble of snow and skis; then abruptly there is nothing. No sound, no sign of Cass. I stand there staring down at the drop that has swallowed her. The snow continues to fall as if nothing has happened.

6 call out

SATURDAY, 5:45 PM: CHIC

"Listen, Chic, if there's an emergency call, no prob. As you know we're just around the corner and can be back instantaneously. I don't want to take calls in a crowded and noisy place. So it's up to you, bro. Any concerns?" Josh gives me a big-brother look.

I guess not. Anyone can take a call, right? So no reason to feel uptight. The guys depart, leaving me alone with their soggy clothes.

So here I am — Saturday night, and I'm sitting in our cramped office over the outdoor gear store. All our high-tech equipment, GPS units, satellite phone, avalanche transceivers, VHF radios — are stored away in a locked safe. We've been broken into before and these bits of equipment cost a fortune. There is also a computer, a chair, and a desk with one wobbly leg. But it's mainly a place to store and dry out our ropes, boots, packs, harnesses . . . you name it. Smells like a skunk wandered in and decided to stay.

I can almost see the steam rising from the crew's most recent droppings. They're a macho bunch, all right. Just wait until the two women who are doing the necessary training join the crew. That'll shake things up. No more wet underwear junked on the floor.

Talking about women . . . My thoughts drift back to the avalanche workshop Josh organized a few weeks back. I kept eyeing this one person. Oversized ski goggles and a toque covered half her face, but the chin jutting out looked kind of familiar. When I saw her loping like a wolf across the snow I knew for sure — it was Cass. I don't see her that often because she's at another school and I'm tied up with my job and studying. But one thing I do know, she's a pro at whatever she does. If it wasn't for her easy-going manner it'd be enough to scare a guy away.

Anyhow, I must have looked distracted because Josh told me, "I get the distinct impression you haven't been listening, Chic. I'm going to partner you up with Cass. Maybe that will help you concentrate for a change?"

And that's how Cass and I ended up as a twosome in the avalanche rescue course. As this was just a refresher course for us, Josh asked us to give the demo. It worked like this. We both were equipped with avalanche transceivers. Another one was turned on, placed inside a pack, and buried somewhere. Our job was to find the pack while everyone else watched. Afterwards they would practise it themselves.

It started out fine. We followed the arrows on our transceivers as they guided us toward the hidden beacon that was transmitting the signal. When we were within a metre or so of ground zero we started moving our transceivers around to find the exact spot. No prob, as Josh would say — we were under his watchful eye so I didn't want to mess things up.

Klutz . . . I dropped the probe I was carrying and looked up a minute later to find Cass standing over the pack.

There was a sparkle in her eyes that echoed in her voice. "I've done this so many times."

"No kidding." As if I hadn't.

The good thing that came out of it was that we decided to head out skiing together — next weekend, to be exact. I'm looking forward to spending the day with her. Let's hope nothing gets in the way.

Josh opens the door again. "Three pieces of fish with your chips?"

"Sure."

"Vinegar and ketchup?"

"Sure."

"You're feeling okay?"

"Sure, I love sitting here by myself on a Saturday night."

"Look, we won't be gone for long. The crew needs to eat. We'll bring your food back."

After the door closes, I pat myself on the back. Good, I actually made my big brother feel guilty over leaving me alone. To tell the truth, I'm happy to be here. Otherwise I'd be at home and my dad would probably be bugging me about studying or doing something useful. That's his favourite word nowadays — useful. Everything has to have a purpose, and running around in the mountains does not make the grade.

But I think that's just a cover-up for something real. You see my dad was caught in an avalanche once while he was backcountry skiing. He made it out, but his best friend wasn't so lucky. He got hung up on a rock when the snow swept over him and they couldn't dig him out in time. My mom says that image sticks with my dad more than the good times in the mountains. So now, with one kid heading a search and rescue team and another a wannabe — it's no wonder he's paranoid, as my mom says. He suspects the worst and keeps coming down hard on Josh for letting me take part in their training sessions. Imagine his reaction when Josh finally says, "You're coming out with us this time, Chic." Doesn't hurt to dream, I guess.

I've barely settled onto the one comfy armchair and opened my book about climbing in Patagonia when my phone goes crazy.

"Chic, it's your dad. I'm just wondering why you aren't home. Your mother has some dinner waiting. Are you all right?"

I can hear her voice in the background, practically dripping with spaghetti sauce. Reminds me I am hungry. "I'm fine, Dad."

"Where are you exactly?"

Long pause. "Josh wanted someone to man the line in their office. We'll be home soon."

In weather like this anyone going into the mountains would have to be an imbecile."

"I know, but . . ." No use arguing against a mind set in concrete. If he didn't carry it to an extreme I'd sort of like the fact that he does worry about his sonny boys. I mean, he could write us off, like some parents I know.

One thing for sure, he's got years of experience in the mountains under his belt. And you gotta respect that.

"Well, I hope your brother won't get called out because of some idiots running around in the mountains during abysmal weather conditions."

"Don't worry, Dad. We're not going anywhere."

I end the call but wait a moment before opening my book, because I'm expecting him to call back. A couple minutes go by and nothing happens. What's wrong — he can't dream up more worries? I flip my book open and lose myself in the Torres of South America — those frost-draped spires bombarded with the worst weather anyone could imagine. One climbing party lived for five days in a mini-bivouac shelter that they kept pulling up a sheer face. I'm at the point where they are worrying about the weight of ice crusting the shelter when my emergency line goes off. A booming voice batters my eardrums, official sounding and definitely not my old man's.

"Corporal Les Murphy, RCMP. We just received a call from the Powder Mountain ski patrol. Two skiers have failed to turn up at the lodge where their friends are waiting. They were supposed to meet around five o'clock. It's now after six, dark and snowing heavily — not the sort of weather to be outside."

I clear my throat, trying not to sound nervous. "Uh . . . any more details?"

"The patrol completed a quick sweep of the area and found barely visible tracks heading out of bounds beyond the patrolled area. Since it is out of their jurisdiction now they have asked us to contact search and rescue. They say weather conditions on the mountain are the worst they have experienced this ski season."

"Right . . ." And I mumble on about something or other as I take notes. My heart is thumping in my ears, drowning out my own voice. I pick up the phone to call Josh. My fingers miss the mark. I try again and finally get through.

7 suicide scarp

"Cass?"

No reply. I call again and again. Suicide Scarp! I whisper the name. I already knew in my gut where we were, but I didn't want to admit it.

Breathe! I pull oxygen into my lungs and try to think. My hands are hooked like claws around the tree. I pull them free and step down to the next tree. Grip it. Move down again. Hug each tree in turn. Creep closer to the edge of the cliff. I can't venture onto the open slope. It's too risky. The whole thing could avalanche.

"Hold on, Cass. I'm coming." Not that I expect her to answer or even hear me.

The slope gets steeper. And the trees further apart. I

lose my grip on one, and for a sickening moment find myself sliding. Reach for a branch. I manage to hold on. But it spins me around and sends me crashing backwards into the next tree. It sways from the impact. I hang there, shaking with the tree. One ski has come loose.

"Cass . . ." I try to make contact. But my mind keeps going over the grim words from the avalanche manual: "Speed is vital." After fifteen minutes buried under snow chances of survival drop drastically.

I wrap one arm more firmly around the tree that stopped my fall. Hope it holds — it's more bush than tree. Somehow I manoeuvre my upper ski around so I'm standing sideways again. I struggle to orient myself in the dim light.

My hands are shaking as I lower myself to the next scraggly tree. I stare down. Falling snow, empty space . . . whatever is or isn't there looks set to swallow me. It's already got Cass.

I let go of the last tree near me and sidestep down. I reach ahead with one pole, feeling my way. I try a trick Cass's parents did when a bunch of us were skiing in a whiteout: I throw a handful of snow ahead of me and watch where it lands. Then I lower myself to that point. I repeat the action, but it's slow going. While trying to hurry I get careless. I sideslip, run into my lower pole, then lose my balance and pitch forward. Snow fills my mouth. I'm falling like in a nightmare. Then everything stops. There is softness below and all around me.

It's quiet. That is, until I start swearing and trying to dig myself out. Snow seeps down the back of my neck, wherever it finds a space. Did I hear a voice? I stop shovelling snow and listen. "Cass?"

A long moment of silence and then, "I can't move."

I don't wait to ask why. She's alive and talking to me. That's all I need to know. I free my arms and start tunnelling until I find both my skis. I'm lucky. If they hadn't come loose I could have a broken leg, maybe two.

"Cass?" I have to make sure that I wasn't imagining her voice.

"Over here."

Untangling my skis is only half the problem. Both ski poles are missing — buried somewhere — and I'll probably never find them. I use one ski to shovel my way out. Finally I'm free of the snow — that powdery stuff I couldn't leave alone.

"Luc . . . over here."

"Keep talking, Cass. I can't see where you are. I'll have to follow your voice." The rock face looming overhead disappears into the falling snow. Not a healthy place for anyone to be.

"Luc?"

"Yes, keep talking. I can't see much beyond my arm in this whiteout."

I'm in a race against the cold and the snow. Without poles I keep sliding back and losing my balance. I stomp one ski hard into the snow. Watch it disappear. Snow has become my worst enemy.

"CASS!" I almost run over her. She's buried to the shoulders. One arm is sticking out like a spindly stick. She tries to move it and moans softly.

I have to move quickly — we're sitting targets here. The cliff and slope above us is being loaded with snow. Even as I watch a thin stream spills over the edge. With my bare hands I start scooping away the snow holding Cass down. If only I had the shovel that I always carry when we go backcountry skiing. Guilt spills over me, like the snow streaming down the cliff.

I clear away the snow from her injured arm and carefully remove the ski pole that is still hanging there. Her other pole is broken, which means neither of us has a useable pair. After more excavating I find her pack. "You have a flashlight anywhere?"

She nods. "Outer pocket."

I retrieve her headlamp and turn it on. The beam slices a wavering line through the whiteout. I clear away more snow and find her skis. Count us lucky — without useable skis you could write us off. I stomp down the snow around Cass. Place her skis side by side to form a platform. "Can you stand there?"

"I keep slipping."

"Hold onto my shoulder while I attach your bindings."

It's done. We both have our skis on and we're both alive. But what now? I lean against the rock face, too wiped to speak or give Cass the hug she deserves.

"Come on, Luc," she says in a voice that sounds faraway. "We have to find shelter somewhere."

Where? Is there any safe place on Suicide Scarp? I'm aware of Cass pulling me. She has a pit bull grip on my hand — it's a good thing she's stubborn. Before it's completely dark we better find something. Don't know what or where. But I'm coming, Cass.

8 first mission

"Josh?

"Speaking. Who's that? I can hardly hear you."

I try to hold the phone steady but still end up shouting. "It's me, Chic. I just got a call from the RCMP."

"Well, go on."

His voice sounds edgy. I try not to stumble over the details. "Two guys are missing on Powder Mountain. They were supposed to meet with friends back at the lodge, but didn't show up."

"How long have they been missing? Have you talked to their friends or the ski patrol? What about weather conditions on the mountain?"

Now it's my turn to sound edgy. "Not so fast, Josh. I

got the call from the RCMP about two minutes ago. You think I've had time to do anything except phone you?"

His voice comes back to me, muffled by chewing sounds. "Good point, Chic. I'll be over right away. In the meantime, talk to the ski patrol. Get their take on the situation up there."

I'm already tapping out their number. Having something concrete to do and knowing Josh is on the way is easing my mind. But how come nobody is answering the phone up there? The ringing goes on forever. Maybe I got the wrong number. I'm about to hang up and try again when a voice comes on, not the ski patrol, but a voice I know from ski trips we've done together.

"Toru? What gives, how come you're answering the phone and not the patrol?"

From the sound of his voice he's equally surprised to hear me. "There was an emergency at the first aid shelter. The ski patrol should be back any minute. You've heard that Luc and Cass are missing? They were supposed to meet us around five and haven't showed up."

"Cass?"

"You know her?"

"Of course I know her. You say she was with Luc?"

"They ski together all the time, sometimes with us,

sometimes alone or with her parents. Luc practically camps on their doorstep."

"Oh . . ." I want to process that piece of information but don't have time right now. "So, what happened? Go on. We have to hurry if they've gone missing."

"Everyone was tired and the weather was getting worse. We kept telling Luc that we should stick together."

"But he didn't listen. What an asshole."

"Look, he's my friend and skiing buddy. I wouldn't call him an asshole. Impulsive, yes."

"Whatever . . . keep going."

He was acting strange this afternoon, like he was out to prove something. He can be stubborn sometimes, but this time he seemed determined to go out of bounds no matter what. And Cass rightly said he shouldn't go alone."

Typical Cass — dragged into something by that impulsive jerk. "Where'd they go?"

"Down Outer Orbit. Nick and I believe they left the patrolled run there. You know where — the usual place."

There's a few seconds of silence when all I can hear is our own breathing. Maybe we both feel a bit guilty about skiing out of bounds even if weather and snow conditions were okay at the time.

"What's the weather doing up there?" I ask, knowing we should get down to basics before Josh arrives.

"Abysmal — it's snowing hard with a complete whiteout higher up. There is zero chance of finding Luc and Cass tonight if they actually are lost somewhere beyond the patrolled runs."

Damn the guy. He puts Cass in danger and makes trouble for everybody, especially Josh. I can practically hear our old man ranting on about those imbeciles who run around in the mountains endangering not only their lives, but the people whose job it is to rescue them.

Josh hurries into the office, balancing a plate of fish and chips in one hand. He grabs the phone from me. I don't appreciate the fact that he almost ripped off my one ear while doing so, but at least he's brought food to his starving brother. He starts rattling off questions, until he realizes it isn't the ski patrol on the other end. When the ski patrol finally does come on the conversation begins to make sense. I listen in while wolfing down my lukewarm dinner.

I can visualize what happened on the mountain. It's the end of the day and the guys are upbeat after the powder run. Toru knows when to quit and Nick will go wherever it's painless and there's food. What can I say about Luc? The guy is stuffed full of complications. I've been with him in the back county — he was a good skier, brought the right gear along, was fun to ski with, didn't do anything rash. But I sure as heck blame him for dragging Cass into trouble. And I gotta admit I'm a bit jealous. How come he gets to ski with Cass all the time?

Josh whacks me on the back and I practically choke on a vinegar-soaked chip. "We're going up the mountain," he tells me. "We? You mean I'm coming along?"

"It's as good a time as any, Chic. We're both here in the office, which means we won't get any flak from the parents, at least not in person and not right away. And it's a plus that you know the people involved."

I wag my head like a dog's tail at each point Josh makes. He's right on. Thoughts of how I'll rescue Cass are already firing away in my brain.

"If conditions don't allow us to head out this evening, at least we'll be ready for an early morning start," Josh says.

While he rounds up the crew, I sort through our equipment. Have to say my hands are shaking. There's a for-sure pile — stuff like ropes, slings, carabiners, a high-tech stretcher that is light and easily assembled, GPS units. . . I throw in a rope ladder, because I made it myself and haven't had a chance to use it yet. Not sure about all the equipment, I'll leave the rest to my big brother.

Josh comes charging back with a bunch of eager guys reeking of fish and chips. Half an hour later we've loaded packs with everything I set out plus helmets, headlamps, first-aid kits, space blankets, and extra food rations — a crew of highly trained search and rescue volunteers all set to go.

Nobody gives me a second look. Josh doesn't bug me more than usual. I'm just one of the guys. And it's an amazing feeling, heading out on my first mission. Correction. I feel nervous knowing Cass is missing on the mountain and wondering if I really am up to being part of the team. Like Josh said, maybe the fact that I know the guys involved will help. I sure hope so.

Josh pats me on the back as we head out the door. "We know you look great in that helmet, Chic. But contrary to what some of you might think it's not compulsory while I'm driving."

The others are laughing. Me? I feel my face dissolving into red. In the rush I'd forgotten to take off the new helmet I was trying out for size. We pile into Josh's beat-up truck. As usual I'm stuffed into the mouldy corner where he stores his spare tire and tools. Seven-thirty and we're on the way.

9 bivouac shelter

SATURDAY, 6:20 PM: LUC

It's weird being in a white world, where you can't see a thing. Snow is everywhere — in the air, on the trees. It flies into our nostrils when we breathe and into our mouths when we talk. Without the narrow beam of Cass's headlamp we'd be as good as smothered by this whiteout. Every few minutes the cliff above us pours snow onto our ledge. Ledge? How wide it is or where it'll take us, I have no clue.

"Don't let go of my hand, Luc. We have to stick together."

"Sorry, Cass." Sorry is the word that's stuck in my mind now. Snow melts on my outstretched palm. No heavy gloves anymore, because they were ripped off when I fell, and I can't go looking for them in a white-out. Like Cass said, we need to stay together and find shelter. I'm lucky to have ended up with nothing worse than a twisted neck.

Cass comes to a stop and probes ahead with her one pole. "I don't think the ledge is continuous."

If I felt nauseous after drinking that beer Nick gave me I feel worse listening to Cass now. So we're stuck on Suicide Scarp. I can't let on how freaked out I am.

She aims her headlamp at the rock face. "It's over-hanging. We should be able to shovel out some snow and crawl underneath."

"Probably." Trouble is, my mind is programmed onto a calamity track. What if we manage to tunnel inside, then snow slides down and blocks the entrance? Or worse still, it suffocates us while we're sleeping.

"*Luc* — I only have one working arm, remember? I need some help digging."

"Sorry, give me a second to get my skis off."

Instantly I sink into snow over my knees. I wade through the bottomless stuff to where Cass has already excavated a sizeable hole. Maybe she's onto something.

"Take a break, Cass. I'll dig."

The snow slips through my hands, sifts back into the hole. Without a proper shovel, I'm getting nowhere fast.

Cass takes over again and seems to do more with one arm than I do with two.

"I've hit rock," she says, directing her headlamp onto the frozen ground beneath the overhang. "There's a dusting of snow there, blown from the outside. It won't bother us."

Together we crawl into our overhang, cave, whatever you want to call it. The snow stops. What I mean, it's no longer falling on us. Outside the snow is still sluicing down. I reach up and touch the rock overhead. It feels solid enough. Any moisture in the cracks will be frozen. No danger of rock chunks falling on our heads unless we had a real blaze going. And seeing as I didn't pack my emergency kit — no matches, no candles, no fire starter, there's no chance of that. "Stupid, all right."

"What?"

"I was just thinking of all the stuff I carry when we're backcountry skiing."

"Well, you don't have it now. And like my unflappable mother says, quit crying over spilt milk."

"You don't say."

"Well, it's true, isn't it?"

"Uh, Cass . . . you don't have a candle or matches by any chance, do you?"

"I always carry a few matches and I have a space blanket too."

While Cass empties her pack I sort out my own junk — a sweater that I took off earlier in the day, an almost-empty water bottle, a lunch bag with chocolate and granola wrappers inside, some ski wax and that's about it. I turn to Cass. "You found anything useful?"

She hands me an unused emergency candle and a small box of matches. "I should have refilled the box. It's been in my pack for ages."

I open the box. Only twelve matches. I take one and strike it against the box. It makes a small spark, but not enough to light the candle. I draw another match out. Same thing. I get Cass to shine her headlamp on the box. The side looks rubbed clean. I try striking a match against the rock where it seems driest. No luck. Everything I try just eats up the matches. I'm left with exactly two.

"Let me try, Luc."

"Wait, I've got an idea."

My hands are shaking as I open up the serrated blade on my Swiss army knife. I've done this before. It's our best chance. I take the two matches, thinking two are less likely to break than one, and draw them across the jagged edge. It works — they burst into flame. I grab the candle from Cass and hold the flame to the unused wick.

There's no wax there. It won't catch. I hold the matches against the wax, trying to melt some. The matches burn my finger, then snuff out. "Oh shit!" I drop the blackened ends and stomp on them.

"It's not your fault, Luc, the matches were old."

"It *was* my fault, dammit." The sound runs around the rock and rebounds on me. "Sorry, Cass, I'm not mad at you, just mad at myself."

I watch her unfolding the space blanket. "Seeing as we're stuck here for the night, we better make ourselves comfortable."

Comfortable? What a laugh. "By tomorrow morning we'll be out of here," I tell her.

"I hope so."

Though Cass doesn't complain, I know her arm hurts whenever she moves. Whatever incredible energy kept her going all this time is fading fast. The first thing I do is spread out the space blanket and put one pack on top. That'll act as insulation between us and the cold rock. We can lean against the other pack. Cass tries to sit down, but falls sideways. Our stiff and heavy ski boots don't help. I drag her to a sitting position, then ease down beside her.

There's rock overhead, behind us, beneath us. Beyond the overhang entrance where our legs are stretched there is snow. Even my voice feels smothered. I'm grateful when

Cass stirs. What she says is not brilliant, but it breaks the silence. "I'm glad we have this space blanket."

"Me too."

We stretch the end over our legs and partway up our chests. It rustles like dead leaves when we move.

"Luc . . . I'm a bit scared. And worried, thinking about my parents. They used to be with search and rescue, years ago. So they know exactly how bad conditions can be in the mountains. They'll go crazy with worry."

I'm scared too. But I can't afford to say it out loud.

"If the weather doesn't clear it'll be too dangerous for a search party. We'll have to find our own way out." She sounds miserable.

"You forget Toru. He'll have called for help. Like I said, one uncomfortable night here and that'll be it."

I'm half believing my own words until my fingers touch the space blanket — it's as skeleton thin as my own confidence. We settle ourselves down for a long night.

10 stalled

SATURDAY, 8:25 PM: CHIC

As we head up the mountain the rain gives way to snow and then blinding whiteout conditions. The driving is so iffy that I'm almost wishing I did have a helmet on. Talk is minimal until we reach the ski patrol cabin. Toru intercepts us at the door and can't quit talking. Finally my brother pushes past him to where the head ski patrol honcho is waiting. Now I'm stuck with Toru. At least I'll get the whole story — but where to focus as he rolls on and on?

"I kept telling Luc we should stick together — weather deteriorating, everyone tired, end of the day, eighty percent of the accidents happen then . . ."

I'm nodding my head; no chance to open my mouth.

Sure, sure. You're absolutely right, Toru. I can just picture Luc — his eyes narrowing, his jaw clenched. He hates being lectured. It brings out every obstinate prickle on his body.

Now Toru has started to list all the what-ifs and there are no end of these for the obsessive worrier. What if they went too far, what if they had a bad accident, what if the weather doesn't clear, what if they develop hypothermia . . . It's all possible, of course, and as Toru goes on and on I get more riled up about Luc's actions. If he wants to take a risk himself, that's one thing, but why involve other people? Why involve Cass?

I tune into my brother's voice as he talks to the ski patrol.

"We'll get them out, it's just a matter of timing. My guess is by tomorrow midday. They can't be that far. If the weather wasn't so ugly, I'd say let's head out now and do a quick recce of the most likely area."

The ski patrol guy points upstairs. "Look, grab a sleeping bag if you need one and find yourself a bunk You'll need some shut-eye before heading off in the morning."

Toru and Nick are all set to stay, too, but the ski patrol not-so-politely nudges them out the door and tells them to go home. I collar them as they're attaching their skis. "You'll contact Cass's parents? Being so involved with skiing themselves they'll realize the danger Cass and Luc are facing."

Toru jumps in again. "I phoned them from the lodge. They wanted to come straight up here, but I advised them how risky that could be. I told them the driving conditions were terrible and that search and rescue was on the case."

"What about Luc's parents? I don't know them."

"None of us do, really. And that probably includes Luc himself. His parents are always somewhere else. Nick and I got no answer at their house. But if and when they do find out about Luc they may demand the impossible — like hiring a fleet of army helicopters. Just kidding."

I roll my eyes. Just what we need — frantic parents. I'm thinking of my own folks who we haven't talked to yet. "Try and calm everyone down, okay?"

"I'll try. If it's not too late when Nick and I get down, we'll phone everyone again."

I'm halfway into the cabin and keen to leave the weather behind when Toru catches me again. "You know the terrain where Luc and Cass were heading. And maybe the others don't, at least not so well. If anyone can find them I think it's you, Chic."

It's ten-thirty and I'm finally climbing onto an upper bunk. Josh and I talked to our parents and dad's voice is still sounding in my ears. "Chic is with you, Josh? I can't believe that you would even consider taking him along. You realize that you are responsible for him."

All the more reason to prove to Josh that I can pull my own weight. The boards on which my skinny foamie is resting creak and groan every time I turn. The guy below has pounded the boards, telling me to quit thrashing about.

So here I am, lying rigid on my back, nose sticking soundlessly into the night air. Wish I could say the same for the guy next door. His nose is whistling like he has a steam engine parked inside. I reach across and flip the sleeping bag liner over his nostrils, hoping to smother the sound. Wrong. Now the engine is going full blast, interrupted every few seconds by watery snorts. I plug my ears with Kleenex.

I get up to pee and shine my headlight on my brother's face. He's sound asleep with a cherubic smile across his face. All that's lacking are wings poking from the sleeping bag. Who could not like this brother of mine?

"Turn off that damn headlamp," a voice growls.

I'm back in bed again, lying on my back and still chasing sleep. Toru's words keep swirling in my head: *If anyone can find them, I think it's you, Chic.* That's a heap of responsibility on my head; this is my first rescue mission.

And it's feeling too personal. I know everyone caught up in this action — especially one person.

"Cass, you're on my mind right now," I whisper to the darkness. *If there's one thing I do in my life I'm going to find you. I don't know exactly where you fit in, Luc.* And that's all I remember before sleep knocks me out.

11  hypothermia

SUNDAY, 2:00 AM: LUC

I wake up with a start. I hadn't meant to drift off, but it's near impossible to stay awake. Cass and I have to fight the cold and the only way we can do this is by moving — our feet, legs, whatever works. I grope around, find the headlamp and shine it on Cass's face. She blinks her eyes.

"Not really asleep," she says, her voice slurring.

I don't like the sound. "How are you feeling, Cass?"

"Cold."

"Look, we have to keep moving, talking — anything to keep awake."

"Sleepy."

Why is it when you most need to talk you can't find anything to say? I try to retrieve an old joke but forget the punchline. Cass doesn't notice. And she doesn't seem to hear the sudden *whumph* of snow nearby. I do. I shine our headlamp at the entrance, or what was the entrance. It's mostly blocked by snow that slid down the cliff face. I aim the headlamp toward the small opening that's left and all I can see is snow swirling around in the narrow beam. *Snow* . . . I must have said the word out loud, because something has made Cass stir again. I hear her moaning softly.

"Arm hurts."

And of course I don't have anything to help her, because my first-aid kit is sitting at home. After kicking myself around again like a worn-out soccer ball, I start trying to be useful. "Cass, I want to take another look at your arm."

"No use."

"Just a quick look."

I can tell by her voice that the slightest movement hurts. No wonder. Her arm feels hot and in one place the bone seems to have broken the skin. With the headlamp wobbling around it's hard to see and I don't want to take off her jacket because of the cold.

"Careful."

By mistake I must have joggled her arm while rolling down the jacket sleeve. Talk about a lethal combo — first the freezing cold and now the heat radiating from a swollen arm. Could an infection be taking hold, this soon, I wonder? Damn it all, I'm not a doctor. All I have is first aid. Come daylight, we *need* to be out of here.

I stop talking to myself and check the time — two o'clock. At least five more hours of darkness, given the weather. I try to make a game out of moving each foot, leg, whatever Cass can manage without it hurting too much — you put your left leg out and shake it all about. Not that this makes us any warmer, but it helps keep us awake. We're like little kids again and about as helpless.

Two hours later and we're still fighting sleep. Heads slip onto chests, jerk back up — same thing over and over. I pull Cass closer, trying to keep her warm. Her head rests on my shoulder. Another time, another place, and I'd be dreaming of this moment. Now I'm just desperate to stay awake and fight off the cold. Hypothermia — it's my biggest fear.

My thoughts zero in on the worst-case scenario — snow keeps falling, rescue crew can't launch a full-out search because of avalanche danger, whiteout conditions prevent a helicopter flyover that could pinpoint our position. In other words, we could be stuck here for a long time.

And worse — with each thump of falling snow I imagine us buried alive, like the two young skiers whose story was all over the newspapers. They dug themselves a snow cave and the roof collapsed while they were sleeping. They suffocated.

"What was your best-ever trip?" Cass's sudden question from the darkness catches me by surprise. What got her started? Did she read my mind?

"Um, hard to say. Maybe that three-day ski traverse near Whistler with you and Toru and his friend, Chic."

"I remember. Chic cooked dinner."

"You do? What I remember is the powder snow and the sunshine and the mountains with no tracks, just waiting for us." I stop when I hear Cass deep breathing. I'll let her sleep some, not too long.

By leaning forward and stretching one arm I can clear away some of the snow blocking the entrance to the overhang. The world outside there looks a shade lighter. Seven o'clock. It's a dismal morning, all right. I'll give it a few more minutes before heading out. I fasten my boots that were undone so the blood could circulate, and pull my jacket hood tighter. Cass is still sleeping. I tuck the space blanket that has come loose under her legs again. She doesn't stir.

Aah . . . body so stiff I can barely crawl on my hands and knees. I manage to wedge my shoulders through the entrance, pushing away snow on the way only to have more collapse onto my back. As I uncurl into a standing position my muscles cry out. What I see outside makes me want to cry, too. There's snow coming sideways, there's snow sliding off the cliffs, there's snow trying to find a way down my neck — the stuff is everywhere. And I can tell you exactly what's happening. It's a stalled weather system and the bad weather could stick around for days.

So I've landed us on a ledge that is collecting snow from every direction. It's a miracle that Cass managed to navigate us here without anyone falling over the edge. When I look below all I can see are a few lonely treetops, their heads floating above empty space or the whiteout — whichever it is.

I want to shout and swear, but my throat muscles pinch shut. I throw snow over the edge. Stomp out a track in the snow. Anything to kickstart my brain. One thing is clear. If we sit around here, waiting for a rescue, hypothermia will come looking for us. Maybe it'll happen so gradually we won't even notice the cold taking over. We'll just sit here, growing colder and colder as the minutes tick by. Two little ice statues frozen in place.

I crawl back under the overhang, collapsing more snow on the way. Cass has moved. The space blanket lies crumpled at her feet.

"Couldn't find you."

I hold her hands against my chest, trying to warm them. Her face tells me how much it hurts when the blood starts to move. She doesn't deserve this.

"I went outside to see what the weather was doing."

"Worried."

She looks very pale and not like the strong Cass I know. I don't want to tell her yet what I'm thinking — that if nobody finds us by late morning, I'm going for help. It'll mean leaving her on her own, but what's the choice? All I know is she needs help soon.

Before sitting down again I scrounge around inside my pack and discover a few loose nuts and raisins. I hand them to Cass.

"Not hungry."

"Eat."

She chews slowly, eyes half shut. I hand her the water bottle that has a few swallows left. Afterwards, I watch her head drop onto her chest. She's asleep again. If the weather wasn't so bad and if we weren't trapped in this out-of-the-way place, I would wait for a rescue party. But I keep asking myself the same question over and over — what's the chance of anyone finding us here?

12 enroute

SUNDAY, 6:30 AM: CHIC

"Uppy-time!" My brother's voice. Hands shaking my sleeping bag. Cold air snaking around my feet. Still dark. "Time to rise and shine."

My half-asleep fingers grope for a flashlight. Focus it on the face leering down. "You could wake me in half-decent English," I grumble.

"I did a pretty good job. You're awake."

"I'm awake all right."

Similar groans from around the room, and the sound of sleeping bags being unzipped. I press my face against the window nearby, trying to make sense of the outside world. Snow plastered there slips down in a sheet, exposing the darkness beyond. It's six-thirty. There won't be much to see until seven or eight. I think of Cass and Luc, especially Cass. What a world to be lost in.

My feet slide off the upper bunk, land on the sleeping bag below, then crunch onto cold floor. Swear words fly from the sleeping bag. "Hey, you didn't like the wakeup call?" He gets no sympathy from me. I'm still half-asleep myself. Altogether, it's not a morning to crow about.

But wait a sec. I sniff the cold air. Hmm . . . the smell of food seeping through the cracks in the floor, the rattle of dishes. It's Josh fixing some eats. That's more like it, big bro of mine. For the moment I forget the world outside, the job ahead of me. I throw on some clothes and stagger towards the stairs. Half-asleep zombies are flowing down the steps and cascading into the kitchen light. They come to life there and tuck into porridge, bacon and eggs, toast, jam, and coffee.

"Eat up, guys," Josh says, "You're going to need it. Weather report calls for continual snow fall, with temperatures easing upward and increased avalanche danger. We couldn't have it much worse."

When Josh says something like that it must be bad. We nod our heads as we chow down our food. What is there to say? It's impossible to think rationally on an empty stomach.

Breakfast over, Josh opens the door a crack to give a preview of what's lurking outside. Snow swirls in uninvited, hits the floor, and melts. Lights from the ski resort waver and look faraway in the falling snow. Watch snow long enough and it can make you dizzy. Great for skiing and boarding, but as Luc has found out, sometimes deadly. Even though it's a rotten attitude for a search and rescue type, I can't help feeling pissed off at Luc. *You should have told him to get lost, Cass. Of course you wouldn't.*

"Shut that bloody door," a voice growls.

"Relax, I simply wanted to educate the crew as to what we're up against."

Groans from everyone. As if we didn't know.

Josh has us checking our gear, wearing his usual sadistic grin as our packs swell. By the time we're finished, our packs must weigh well over 15 kilograms each. Before stepping out the door we check that our avalanche beacons are operating and our VHF radios are on the same frequency. My GPS is stashed in an outside jacket pocket.

Already I can feel the sweat trickling down my face. Probably because I'm wearing the thermal underwear my dad gave me for Christmas. It's overkill, but that's my dad for you. And being a bit hyper sure gets the sweat flowing. I keep thinking of Cass. It was cold in the cabin overnight. What was it like outside? No tent, no sleeping bags . . . who knows what those two had along?

We're out the door at last. The freezing air curling over my face and pinching my nostrils shut feels good for the first couple of minutes. We hunker down over our skis, fit boots into bindings, grab poles and head toward the lift. It's a good hour before the scheduled opening and Josh had to rout the operator out of bed.

Josh cruises up beside me and we slip onto the same chair. "How are you doing, Chic?"

"Not half bad."

"Nervous?"

"I'm doing okay." I don't want to admit I'm nervous. Josh expects a lot of me and I've got to live up to his expectations. Admitting I'm really nervous won't help him or me.

"It's challenging conditions for your first outing, Chic, for everyone actually. To tell the truth, I'm not sure how far we'll get this morning."

Hearing this from my usually unstoppable brother is scary. I try to fire a question back, but the cold air catches my breath as the chair speeds up. Snow pummels our faces. I pull my hood tighter and bend over my knees. Right now my dad's state-of-the-art underwear is feeling just fine. By the time we reach the top, we're blanketed with snow. Everything around us — trees, lift shack, even the cables overhead — looks as if it's been transported from the sub-arctic and dropped down here.

Josh waits until the last guy is off the chair, then flaps us forward. I say flap because the wind is tearing at our jackets, like they're sails. With the wind spitting snow from every direction, I catch a few words of his shouted orders, "Follow the ski patrol down."

That's enough to set the eight of us in motion. We're a single unit, controlled by headquarters. Picture a caterpillar weaving its way over rough ground. That's us and I'm at the tail end. My skis make no sound as they carve through the snow. The moguls of a few days ago are buried. One turn flows into another, until I hear the ski patrol shouting over the wind.

"Okay, this is where we believe they cut off the run. Anything beyond the sign here is out of bounds and where search and rescue has to take over."

I slide to a stop and stare at the sign that creaks ominously back and forth in the wind. *Out of Bounds. Area Not Patrolled*, it reads. I hold the rope with one hand. Still whiteout conditions — I can't see more than a few metres ahead.

Josh taps my arm and blasts me with a loud voice. "Chic, you know the terrain here. You've skied the gully with Luc or one of his friends."

"No need to advertise the fact that I've skied out of bounds," I mumble.

"What I mean to say is that you have skied here before and I haven't. So I'd like you to start off breaking trail."

"Okay." Trust Josh to twist the guilty knife. Yes, I have skied out of bounds here — in decent conditions. Just don't mention my name in the same breath as Luc's.

"Let's head off, then. Find the gully and check it out — that's our first move. If we don't locate the two skiers there, we'll need to do some serious rethinking before venturing out further in these weather conditions."

After watching the ski patrol disappear down the run, I go past the rope marking the ski area boundary. It's another world out here. For one thing, my skis are in free fall once they hit the untracked powder. Most of the time I can't even see them as I push forward. No wonder there are no tracks visible from yesterday.

After a while I hear Josh behind me. "Step aside, Chic. I want to keep rotating the lead in these difficult conditions."

"I can keep going. I'm not that tired."

"I said step aside, Chic. It's not compulsory that you keep going first." Josh waves his GPS under my nose, reminding me that I'm not the boss here. A line marking our course on the small screen stares me in the face.

"Okay."

No arguing with the search and rescue leader. I step

aside and let the others pass. My skis slip into automatic as I follow the well-beaten track. I keep my eyes open for possible landmarks but everything is buried deep under snow.

I try to imagine the scenario after Luc and Cass took off. Did they ski down the opening and get hurt or caught in an avalanche there? If so, chances are good we'll find them soon, or at least some clue as to what happened. But more likely they strayed off course. I try to visualize where they might have gone wrong, where we should concentrate our search. There's a heap of rugged terrain beyond the groomed runs.

And always I rebound to the big *why. Cass — you could have said no. And Luc — you could have turned around if she wouldn't let you go alone. Are you that stubborn? Or selfish maybe? Just tell me why, man.*

13 desperate move

SUNDAY, 10:00 AM: LUC

For the longest time Cass sleeps, her head leaning against my shoulder. Our snow cave is feeling more and more like a tomb, it's so quiet. Even the wind is a faraway whisper. Every few minutes I hold a finger beneath Cass's nose to make sure she's breathing. I feel her cheek for any warmth. I want her to sleep some, but not too long. I keep asking myself what I should do.

Cass wakes with a jerk and lifts her head from my shoulder. She smiles as if nothing is wrong.

"You've been asleep for quite a while. I was going to wake you."

"Sleepy."

"You should move some."

"I should?"

"Yes."

I help her to move her good arm and each leg. What a struggle, it's as if she doesn't care. I end up doing most of the work. "Come on, Cass, swing your arm."

"Swing."

"What?"

"Something else . . ." Her voice trails off.

Where is she, anyhow? Now I'm truly scared. "Hypothermia." The word I whisper echoes around the cave.

"Hmm . . ." Cass mumbles things I can't understand and her head drifts onto my shoulder again.

I check my watch — 10:00 am. By now they could be out searching for us. Question is, how long should I stick around here, hoping someone will find us? I don't think Cass can last through another night. Checking my watch every few minutes becomes an obsession — 10:15 . . . 10:30 . . . 10:45. If anyone *is* out there in this weather where would they be now? Knowing Toru, he'll have passed on more than enough info to the searchers. That should help us.

By 11:15 I've had enough of waiting around. It's time to stir. Without waking Cass, I crawl from the overhang and have a listen. No sound except snow pinging against my jacket. I cup my hands and shout into the air. The snow stifles my voice. Unless somebody was standing directly overhead there's no way they could hear or see me. And seeing as nobody is there, I guess the next move is mine.

With cliffs above me and a ledge that goes nowhere, I'm left with exactly one choice. I don't like the choice. It's not smart to head down, but I have to. At least gravity will be helping. I tunnel my way to where the ledge runs out and look over. A few scraggly fir trees stare back at me. But the good news is there's snow clinging to the slope, which means it's not a sheer rock face. It'll go I figure.

Now comes the tough part — breaking the news to Cass. I crawl back under the overhang where Cass is asleep, her head tilted against the bare rock. She opens her eyes when I sit down. "Funny dream . . ."

Her voice stalls me. Can I really leave her here alone? I seesaw back and forth — stay here, leave. If she doesn't get help soon the cold will tunnel into her body like some deadly worm. I shake my head, trying to get rid of that image. What's more likely: search and rescue getting here in time or me finding my way down? "I don't know. I just don't know."

I lean my head on the rock, searching for the right answer. I must have dozed off because I wake with a jump. I check my watch: 11:40. It's dark by six in this weather. If I'm going to go I need to go now.

"Cass." I lean close until I feel her breath on my cheek. "Cass, I have to leave now. I'm going for help."

Without opening her eyes she whispers the last word I said, "Help."

And that's all. Not another word. Did she understand or was she just repeating a word? I take off my sweater, the only thing keeping me warm, and slip it around her head and shoulders. It'll shield her from the cold rock. All I have left now is a light vest and shirt under my jacket. If I don't keep moving I'll chill out within minutes.

I don't look back while crawling from the cave. But her pale face follows me wherever I turn. Maybe she isn't aware I'm leaving. Outside, I grab my skis and fasten them together so they won't run away on me. With a pole in one hand and skis in the other, I plow a path to where the ledge drops off. Difficult to judge, but it could be fifteen metres down to the next ledge and yet another cliff below that. Figures — this whole area is a maze of cliffs and ledges.

"Hold it!" I've forgotten the basics. Nobody stands a chance of finding Cass unless I leave a sign behind. But what? No point stamping HELP in the snow. We're too hemmed in here and falling snow would only wipe it out. The other problem is I've left most of my stuff behind with Cass.

"Wait — I've still got my red ski hat." I grab my toque and wave it around like I'm celebrating a victory. Now to figure out where to put the hat — it has to be visible from above and below. I go crazy, trying to find a spot to hang the darn thing. That's when I stumble over one of our broken ski poles. I ram it into the snow and fasten my toque on top. It's the best I can do.

I start kick-stepping my way down. So far the bushy trees near the top are holding the slope together. Then one step gives way beneath my feet. I manage to grab a single tree part way down the slope. The impact rips the light gloves I'm wearing and cuts my hand. But I've stopped and so has the snow. "Whew . . ."

I carry on kick-stepping. Force myself to go slow. I can't risk an accident when I'm alone. One boot sinks out of sight and gets snagged between rocks. I manage to wrestle it free and continue creeping down. A rock bulge raises its ugly head from the snow beneath me. I turn, face into the slope and somehow wangle my way over the rock. Then it's clear sailing to the ledge below. I let myself slide the remaining metre or so onto terra firma.

"*Yes!*" I'm onto the ledge and it looks promising. Except for the blood dripping from my cut I'm in pretty good shape. I drag some toilet paper from my jacket pocket and wrap it around my hand. It's the best I can do.

I scrape the snow off my skis and step into the bindings. After the boot wading I've been doing, skis feel good. I follow the ledge in the general direction of where the ski hill should be. This works until the ledge slopes upwards and my skis start slipping. I back track to recce a chute that I'd written off as too steep. A single tree juts from the snow, halfway down. Below, it looks steeper yet. I test the snow at the top, setting off a small slide. Okay, less snow to worry about.

I sidestep at first, feeling ahead with my pole and moving carefully. The single tree is coming up below me. It might be smart to take off my skis now, but fiddling with equipment only wastes time. I manage to manoeuver my lower ski around the tree, and I'm lifting the upper ski when the tip snags a buried branch. I go flying.

No time to think or do anything. I'm cartwheeling down the slope, snow swirling like a river around me. There's a sickening crunch as one ski tip hooks a snow-covered boulder. My binding flies open. The ski takes off. I come to rest half buried in snow. Alive, but stupid, *stupid* — the one word that sits on my tongue.

14 the gully

SUNDAY, 9:00 AM: CHIC

Josh is still breaking trail. You'd think he was walking on air and not wallowing in close to a metre of powder snow. Can he keep it up? Knowing his fitness level — not to mention he's as stubborn as our old man — the answer is yes. He stops when we reach an opening in the trees, turns around and waves a ski pole in my direction, "I'm guessing this is your opening, Chic?"

I nod my head. But why my opening? I only skied it once, to tell the truth, and that was enough. I'm not in the same league ski-wise as Cass or Luc, and maybe some of my dad's caution has rubbed off on me. "I don't think we're going to find them here," I mumble.

"We have to check the closest and most obvious area, first. That's how it works, Chic." End of discussion.

What I wanted to get across is this — I think we're wasting time looking for Cass and Luc here. They are both top skiers. If they did find the opening they'd likely be home free. My hint falls flat on its face. I'm the young and inexperienced kid brother, here thanks to Josh. I keep my mouth shut.

A moment's break and everyone is busy — adjusting ski bindings, taking a quick slurp of coffee and wiping off goggles. Josh has untied his shovel, same as the ones we all have attached to our packs, and is digging a snow pit. I join him along with the others and we examine the snow profile. Depending on how the different layers look, it'll give us some idea of the slope stability and whether it's likely to avalanche.

"Of course the snow pack is way too heavy," Josh says finally, "but at least the new stuff is not sitting on top of an icy layer. Can we swear it's a hundred-percent safe? You never can." He shakes his head.

Everyone but Josh has managed to choke down some food. It's typical for him to forget food when he's focused. "Eat," I say, handing him an energy bar.

He stuffs it inside a pocket and gives us a briefing. "If weather was reasonable and we had more manpower, I'd split up our crew at this point — one group ski down the gully, the other carry on further. Not today. We'll stay together and head down the opening. Go slow and keep well spread out. We'll stop partway down. Any questions?"

"Above the chute is a good place to stop," I tell him.

"Right, let's move. Chic, you head off with Finn and Roc. I'll recheck avalanche beacons as everyone goes by."

I ski past Josh, hearing the familiar ping of the avalanche beacon against my chest. I pat it like it's a best friend, zip up my jacket again, and I'm off.

The snow swallows my skis and flies into my face with each turn. There are no ski tracks ahead of us, no signs of life. I'm nervous, all right, but it's hard to resist the whisper of the snow: *Go faster . . . faster.* The space between Finn and me grows. "Slow down," he shouts. I make my turns wider and force myself out of the fall line.

When we reach the point where the slope narrows into a chute, we stop. Once in the chute you're there for keeps, until you reach bottom. I look down. "Uh . . . oh, we've got a problem." The top section has been gouged by an avalanche and we can't see where it ends because of falling snow.

Josh stops beside me. "It's a small slide. But it does make you wonder what set it off."

"You don't think ..." One look at the rest of the tight-lipped crew shuts me up. Doom and gloom scrawled there, for sure.

The good news is we have less snow ourselves to worry about. I can understand now why Josh wanted to check out this area first. All I can do is hope no one got caught up in the slide. Cass is too smart for that, I tell myself. Smart? What's that got to do with it when you're following some idiot? You have to be lucky — period.

"Everyone ready? Then let's go," Josh says.

This time I'm at the end of the pack. I sit back on my skis and follow the tracks. The problem is we have to check out Cass and Luc's every possible move and it all takes time — too much time.

I hit the avalanche debris in the run-out zone. My skis go wild, wobbling all over the place, before I come to a stop. Roc has faced off with a block of snow and takes a nose dive. I help him up.

"You okay?"

"Sure ..." Mumbled swear words.

We join the rest of the crew who are checking out the avalanche tongue. We know that Luc and Cass weren't carrying avalanche transceivers, so ours are no help. Over and over our avalanche probes slice through the snow. Every time they come up empty.

Finally Josh straightens up. "That's it guys, we've covered the whole area and found nothing. Take a break."

A long sigh of relief as we suck air in and let it heave out. I kick at the snow that has frozen into solid chunks. A few stray tree branches caught up in the swirl of snow litter the surface. That's my worst nightmare — being buried in an avalanche and trying to claw a breathing space around my face before the snow freezes. Be vigilant if you must go skiing after a heavy snowfall, our old man is always warning his sonny boys. Repeat often enough and it hopefully rubs off.

I hear Josh's voice drifting into my world. "We'll regroup back at the lodge and have a quick coffee while we wait for our support group to arrive. Four more guys, one of them a paramedic, puts us at a more reasonable number."

We leave the avalanche debris behind us and eventually cruise to a stop on the Far Easterly run. A few cross-country types sail past us. They aren't even breathing heavily. I slog sullenly after them until a whiff of food from the lodge hits my nostrils. I lunge forward and forget about muscle-bound skate-skiers. The ski lodge is two minutes away. But all the while I'm remembering we're a long way from finding Cass and Luc.

15 another go

SUNDAY, 10:30 AM: CHIC

I stare through the snow-battered windows of the lodge. The diehard skiers are out there, but I don't see huge line-ups at the lift. I gulp down my hot chocolate while the other guys drink coffee that smells like it's been sweating over a burner since breakfast. I feel a hand on my shoulder.

"Chic."

"Toru, what gives?"

"I had to come up. How is it going?"

"Nothing to report. We'll be heading out again — soon as the new crew arrives. Where's Nick?"

"I don't know and right now I don't care. You heard what he did? He bought a large beer for Luc and pressured him into drinking it. We all know Luc doesn't drink."

"Nick did?"

"My parents told me the beer probably clouded Luc's judgment — their words, not mine. I doubt that's true, but I got a nonstop lecture from my dad anyhow."

"Talking parents, did you get in touch with Cass and Luc's folks?"

"I phoned everyone. Cass's parents drove me up this morning. They want to help."

"How?"

"I don't know. Naturally they'd like to get out there and search for their daughter, but they live in the real world. They know they can't."

"Is that them coming along with Josh? I've never met her folks."

"That's her parents, all right. You can tell by their worried look."

So that's what has been keeping Josh. He's hurrying toward us with his "I'm ready for anything and nothing's going to stop me" look. Two people are stuck to his side. I listen in on the conversation. "If we can be of any help . . . we brought our skis along just in case and we both have industrial first aid."

"That's great. Just being up here and being so supportive is wonderful. And when we do find them, it'll help your daughter no end."

I'm hearing my brother, the diplomat, zigzagging his way through a dicey situation. And I'm in awe. His phone goes as he is about to speak to me. The voice on the other end is loud enough for me to hear. "Is that search and rescue?"

"Yes."

"I'm calling long distance and I want to know what's being done about my son, Luc, who I understand is missing. What's going on up there? You aren't out looking for him at the moment. Why not? Have you brought in a helicopter to search for him? I'm concerned about my son and —"

Josh again. "I understand how concerned you must be. We are too. We have searched the most obvious areas and are waiting for more search and rescue personnel to arrive. Unfortunately weather conditions don't allow for a helicopter overflight."

"I'll phone again and I trust you will have some more substantial news for me."

"You are welcome to come up."

"That's impossible. My wife and I are away on business."

End of conversation.

Josh turns to me shaking his head. "The voice was so loud I guess you overheard. How some people react, eh?"

"No kidding."

The crew has rallied around Josh. "We'll meet at the lift in ten minutes," he tells us.

Everyone nods in silent agreement. We polish off coffee, hot chocolate, freshly baked cinnamon buns dripping with brown sugar, and listen in. "I just got the up-to-date forecast. With luck we'll have a break in the weather before the next low pressure system moves in this evening. We have to move fast. Another night out for those two would be serious."

No need to say more. The team springs into action. Jackets, gloves, and helmets on, packs retrieved from the rental office, and we're outside again, tasting snow on our faces.

The extra search and rescue volunteers that Josh has called in from another area meet us at the lift. There's no time for long introductions. Josh gives us a quick briefing before we head up. "We'll repeat our route of this morning, but concentrate on the area beyond the opening. In order to cover more ground we'll work in three groups. Sound reasonable?"

A rhetorical question, as my dad would say. Sure, it's reasonable. It has to be, because this is my big brother speaking, our search and rescue leader. On both counts he's gotta be right. He has to make the right call before any action. Not that he doesn't listen to his crew, but the simple fact is, he has more hours of experience than the rest of us. I'd never have the guts to be in his boots.

The ski patrol steers our group to the front of the lift line-up as the next chair swings around. The seats are soggy with half melted snow and there isn't time for the lift attendant to brush the stuff off. We lower ourselves onto the chairs and are airborne. I pull down the safety bar and turn towards Josh. "What if weather doesn't change?"

"We'll get our break, no worries. Is our meteorologist ever wrong?"

"Like, fifty percent of the time." As the minutes barrel by I grow more uneasy. We need that break in the weather.

Josh leans closer so I can hear him over the wind swaying our chair. "You know the area, Chic. Any idea where we should concentrate our search?"

"Look, like I told you already, I don't know the area that well. But yes, I have skied there."

"Still, that means you are one up on the rest of us."

"I suppose."

My brother is persistent if nothing else. We've gone over this — how many times? I don't like being nailed down as the expert. I don't have the experience of the others. But hold on — maybe at this exact place and moment in time I am the expert.

"So what do you say, Chic?"

"Well . . . for starters, they're on downhill skis. As we all know that makes it almost impossible to climb back up, especially in deep powder snow."

"Correct. So, likely they were cautious about heading down too steeply."

"For sure — and then missed the opening by staying too high. They realized their mistake and turned around, but it was too late — they couldn't follow their tracks back up. And in whiteout conditions, they'd get more and more confused."

"Sounds plausible."

The scenario that Josh and I have sketched out chills me. There's a long moment of silence as we listen to the wind scouring the snow beneath the lift. Drifts form fingers that try to catch our skis, then collapse, empty-handed. I think of the winter when they had to tunnel out a path for the chairs. Meanwhile, the snow keeps falling.

"If the weather doesn't improve, I can't risk expanding the search too far into the Scarp area," Josh says finally. Not my optimistic brother speaking, but the leader responsible for the safety of his crew.

We're nearing the top of the lift. "I know Dad was mighty upset last night when I told him you were along, Chic, but I think we did the right thing. Don't worry."

Where did that come from? I don't have time to ask. I lift the restraining bar and our skis dangle free. Josh gives my backside a push and we're poling away from the lift area and on our way. His words stick in my ears. Good old Josh — when things look down, he tries to make you feel good. He points his skis toward Outer Orbit and the rest of us follow.

16 search and rescue procedure

SUNDAY, 11:35 AM: CHIC

By the time we reach the cutoff point on Outer Orbit the snow is easing. We ski past the rope and are soon into the trees where ski tracks are still visible. The wind is muffled here, but occasionally a dump of snow from above reminds us the treetops are moving. Luckily, it's not that heavy spring snow, landing on us or there could be serious injury.

So this is our world — a few hours squeezed between storms and darkness, a few hours that are critical for the lives of two people. And how am I doing? Not so uneasy, now that the snow has stopped and we are finally into the area where I think Cass and Luc got lost. Josh is back to normal — hyper, that is, talking weather, equipment, timing, and rehashing old jokes. We call it Josh's tongue lashing. It keeps morale up — the job of any good leader.

"Five-minute stop," he says when we reach the opening.

Packs are thrown off and Thermos bottles opened. Maybe the crew is gulping down coffee, but Josh isn't taking a breather. "We have a break in the weather — four, maybe five hours max. We've got to maximize that time, seeing there's another storm front predicted for tonight. So here's how it stands. We left one crew member down at the lodge to coordinate our search effort and relay any information. The eleven of us left here will divide into three teams and fan out across the search area."

Josh opens a 1:50 000 topographic map of the area and jabs his finger at three different points where the groups will start their search. A plain old map can still be handy. Sometimes I raid my dad's carefully guarded map cupboard for them, which hassles him no end.

In the old days, search and rescue operated without any GPS or VHF radios. Maps, whistles, and loud voices — that was about it for communication, mega-primitive compared to our equipment. And right now Josh is talking radios. "Before we spread out, check that your radios are on the right frequency."

The safety of the whole crew is his first concern. If one group gets into trouble it can sabotage the whole search effort. Because I'm too young to be an official member of search and rescue, it's a given that I stay with Josh. I'm under the brotherly wing, so to speak, and I'd better behave. Lucky for me he has a sense of humour.

I stuff my half-eaten lunch into my pack and start reshuffling the contents. This standing around makes me antsy. What's Josh up to, still checking equipment? I know he's an equipment freak, but right now he seems to be moving in slow motion. I thought we were in a hurry. *Relax, Chic*, I tell myself.

Josh hands me another piece of equipment. "Satellite phone."

"You really think we can find a reliable signal in bad weather and dense bush?" I'm also thinking of the extra weight for my overloaded pack.

"We're taking it, period. And you are responsible for it. Leave a potentially useful piece of equipment behind and we could regret it."

I grumble away to myself as I stuff the satellite phone into my ballooning pack. I have to keep reminding myself who I'm talking to, my search leader and not my brother Josh. I have to negotiate a tricky path between these two different people. Is it hard for him too? Maybe this is why he hasn't taken me along before.

Josh has already forgotten about me and the satellite phone. I hear him talking to the search and rescue volunteers who joined us at the lodge. "Seeing as you're in charge of the rescue sled, I'd like you to stay behind here and cover the area closest to the opening. Be on the ready if and when we need the sled."

As we set off I'm tuning into his final words. "The terrain here is unforgiving. We can't be too careful. Weather and snow conditions are bad enough as is. If in doubt, call me, or if for some reason you can't get through, contact our search and rescue coordinator at the lodge."

After the second group of four drops off, Josh, Roc, Finn, and I carry on. We're searching the area furthest from the ski resort and the groomed runs. It suddenly feels very lonely out here. Will the weather hold? As usual Josh seems to read my thoughts. "We're in luck — take a look at the blue sky overhead."

We peer through the hole in the trees where he's pointing. "Um . . . if you're looking through blue-tinted glasses you might see blue. We all know you have blue-sky syndrome," Roc says.

"Look, it's not snowing and the wind has died down."

As Josh says, we have to go for it while time and

weather conditions allow. I've a hunch we're the group most likely to find Cass and Luc. Why? Because I know Luc always pushes the boundaries. He'd keep going. He would wait until the absolute last minute before admitting he was wrong and turning around.

After marking the present position on our GPS units, we're ready. Josh has his VHF radio in one hand and is making a test call. "Group one . . . group one, SAR base command. Anything to report from your end? Over."

Josh nods his head as he listens quietly. Obviously nothing major to report. He checks in with group two. Now it's back to him. "Roger. We're going to try and head gradually down now. Out."

Josh has finished talking. Now comes the test — guessing how and where two people went wrong. You need a heap of mountain knowledge and some intuition. I take a deep breath. Everything else was leading up to this — the first-aid courses, the rope work, the mock rescue sessions, and Josh's lectures. Am I up to it? Can I keep both my big brother and the search and rescue master happy?

I peel off the skins that were glued onto the bottom of my skis to prevent me from slipping. With those off, I can go full out. We fan across the slope within shouting distance of one another. I'm feeling stronger and working harder than I ever imagined possible. I'm alert to every sound — the drift of snow, a branch cracking somewhere, Josh on the VHF, someone hacking and then spitting onto the snow, the pounding of my own heart.

I've become a wild animal, sniffing out tracks, head down, ears pricked forward. I'm lost in my own world.

17 time enough

SUNDAY, 1:00 PM: CHIC

Josh calls a halt and the three of us join him. He's staring at his GPS and has our old map lying open on the snow. "I believe the slope we are on here becomes too steep for safe going, unless we want to think rope work. If you don't like the look of it as we head down, backtrack. Better to err on the side of caution."

Better to err on the side of caution — another of our dad's choice sayings. But it's also the motto of any search and rescue leader. I try to look at it through Josh's eyes. Go slow and lose our weather opening, speed up and risk an accident. We're squeezed between the two. I check my watch — one o'clock. With luck we have five hours of daylight left.

"Keep your skins handy. We'll be needing them whenever we have to climb back up," Josh says, before we spread out again.

I pole off and within minutes the others are out of sight. If it wasn't for the VHF radio stashed in my pocket I'd sure feel lonely. I'm getting a call right now. It's Roc coming in.

"It's looking gnarly where I am. Problem is the convex slope. I can't see over the bulge to what lies below."

"Finn here. "Same thing — I can't see down. Should we pass on this slope? Over."

Josh's voice. "Most definitely. It's skin time, you three. We'll regroup up here. I haven't heard from you , Chic. Come in."

"Half a minute."

I'm hearing Josh, but I'm not into heading up yet. What lies below me looks too interesting. Like I said, Josh, give me half a minute.

Josh comes in again — heavy breathing as he struggles with a stubborn skin that won't stick onto his skis "Is everyone heading up now? Over."

I nod automatically, but I can barely make out his slurred words. That's excuse enough for me to keep going. I'm focused on sidestepping down the slope. A couple more metres and I should get an idea of what lies below. It'd be dumb to turn back now. I grab a stunted tree, sticking from the snow. Work my skis around more of the little stragglers. Sidestep again. Another half-metre and I'll be able to see down. I lean forward for a look and, "Uh-oh."

My lower ski sinks into a hole where there's a buried tree. I lose my balance and find myself pitching forward. *You've blown it, Chic.*

Not sure how far I've fallen. All I know is I manage to hook one arm around a tree and stop. I lie here shaking, clutching the tree like it's a life jacket. If I rescue myself from this mess, I may need another, drown-proof life jacket when I face Josh.

After picking myself up, I look down. "Whoa, I'm not going there." A few metres below me the slope ends in a cliff.

I stomp out a platform as best I can among the mini-trees. Take off my skis, one after the other and struggle with putting on skins. "Dammit." Because it's cold and I've already used them, the glue won't stick. I press them onto the bottom of my skis and rub my bare hand across the surface. The friction helps.

Josh's voice comes over the VHF again. "Chic, is anything wrong? Roc and Finn are here. We're all waiting. Over."

I drag out my VHF and in the rush almost drop it. "I'm having trouble with skins." True, but not the whole truth.

Seconds tick by. I can't push it. My position is too dicey. The platform I've stomped out isn't much wider than my skis. And there's a cliff gaping like a shark's mouth below me. My skins are finally sticking. *Now go, Chic.* What a wipeout! I'm no closer to finding Cass, plus Josh will be mighty unhappy with me.

Trees block my way forward. I swing my lower ski into a kick turn. *Easy now.* I'm half way around and not much liking the view when I see something. "A broken branch!"

It's a yellow cedar branch, half split and dangling onto the snow. Looks like a recent break. I didn't do it, so who or what? Cedar branches are flexible and can bend with the weight of snow. An animal? I can't think of any animal that would be crazy enough to be here, except two skiers maybe. "Cass! Luc!" I hear myself shouting.

For the longest moment I stand there listening. Not a sound. I focus on the broken branch, willing it to tell me more. It hangs limply from the tree, unmoved by wind, snow, or my voice. But they gotta be somewhere near. Why don't they answer? A hundred reasons race through my head.

I forget about the VHF radio until Josh's voice lands in my lap. "Chic, are you all right? Come in."

"Hold on, I'm coming."

Josh again. "So you say, but nothing materializes."

With skins on I don't need to follow my winding tracks through the trees. I climb straight up, plowing my way through the deep snow. I'm soon standing beside the others, out of breath and with sweat popping like zits from my forehead.

Josh stares me down. "You didn't answer. You didn't follow Roc and Finn when I radioed you. We've been real concerned, Chic. So what's up?"

I'm like a dog that's just peed on the living room rug, but is wagging its tail hopefully. I've done everything wrong. Went off. Didn't clue the others in. Put myself and the group in possible danger. But I did find a hint as to Cass and Luc's location.

I'm partway through my story when Josh bursts in, "Which is why search and rescue isn't keen having you young guys on board. You don't know when to quit." Josh rants on until Roc comes to my rescue and reminds him of the broken branch.

Within seconds Josh is on the VHF radio, informing the other groups that we're maybe on to something here. He marks our present location on the GPS, then opens his topo map and jabs his finger at a point where the contour lines fall all over one another. Move the finger up or down and what you find are cliffs. Yeah, we're next door to the gnarliest section of Suicide Scarp.

For the moment I'm off Josh's radar, but he doesn't forget easily. I have to show him I'm a responsible member of the crew. At the same time I'm kind of pissed off that he hasn't made more of my discovery. I'm not a happy camper.

But I do sharpen my ears to what Josh says next: "We'll try to go around these cliffs. If that doesn't work we may end up having to do a rope descent, all of which takes time. And we don't have much of that left."

I see him glance furtively at the sky which is growing gloomier by the minute. Before we head off, he hands me an energy bar, but doesn't give me his usual brotherly shoulder pat. My mind isn't focused on food. I check my watch yet again. It's pushing two.

18 accident

SUNDAY, 2:15 PM: LUC

"Stupid . . ." The word sounds strange and faraway. Is somebody talking somewhere? I don't know who it is. "Stupid." The same word again. Now I know it's me talking, the word ricochets through every bone in my body. My mouth moves as I say the word.

How long have I been lying here? Don't know. It must be a while, because I'm freezing. I remember falling. That was after I left Cass. I don't want to think further back.

"You want to know how long you've been lying here? Then look at your watch, stupid," I tell myself. I struggle with an arm buried in snow. It hurts, but I manage to lift it. I'm shaking so hard that it spills snow over my upturned face. I lower the arm until it's almost touching my eyes and brush the snow off. The watch is buried under my jacket. I pull the sleeve back with my teeth. *2:15.* Three hours and it'll be getting dark. I have to move.

I'm sprawled on my back, half buried in snow, somewhere on Suicide Scarp. That's what I know. There's plenty I don't know and I'd better find out. I touch a bare hand to my cheek where it hurts. Blood! Jerk the hand away. When I move my head, blood drips onto the snow. Try to cover the gash with my other hand. But the fingers don't work. I panic and start thrashing around.

That's when I figure out my left leg might be broken. For some crazy reason this calms me down. I force myself to deep-breathe. Try to think clearly. I won't give up. I can't — not with Cass back there.

With my good arm, I push myself into a sitting position. I'm gripped by the look of my splayed-out leg, half buried in snow. Move and it sinks out of sight. But the snow has stopped falling. And there's some blue sky overhead. I should move.

"Come on, Luc, quit stalling." My words split the silence and goad me into action. I have one good leg and one workable arm. What else have I got? I look around. Not much.

Wait a minute. I see something sticking from the snow. It's a ski, or what's left of one. And it's within reach. I drag the ski to the surface. The tip is broken; same goes for the binding. But I know it's useable. I've been a volunteer guide for handicapped skiers. If you're short one leg, mini-skis attached to both arms help balance. It's worth a try.

The adrenaline rush of the last few minutes is shutting down. Pain kicks back even harder. All the moving around hasn't helped. I try to concentrate, but the pain is like a fog weighing me down.

I don't move. It feels good just resting. I don't care anymore. The cold doesn't hurt. It kind of sneaks in without advertising the fact. I guess freezing to death isn't the worst way to go.

"Get a hold of yourself, Luc. You're not going to die. Get off your fat ass." I realize I've been shouting. But nobody hears me. Nobody answers.

I struggle onto my one good leg, holding the ski for balance. It's heavy, but it moves nicely through the snow. Provides some flotation, just not enough. I keep sinking. Stop to catch my breath. I've gone about a metre, two at the max. I glance around. The slope looks steeper below me. More cliffs? There's a gully to my left, most likely a stream bed in summer. Not a healthy route to follow, but

I've got no choice. Have to head down and water flows downhill. "Duh."

I wait until the worst pain lets go, and then push forward with one leg. Without a splint my broken leg follows like a clumsy partner. The snow helps to cushion it. I half crawl, half swim through the snow. From habit I check my watch. *3:20*. It hardly matters anymore. I hear water under the snow. It sounds nice. Nothing to drink for a long time. I let some snow melt in my mouth. Still very thirsty. Not hungry.

19 avalanche

SUNDAY, 2:30 PM: CHIC

It seems like we've been going forever, struggling to find our way through this maze of cliffs and ledges. The other groups haven't had any luck either. It's mid-afternoon and we're feeling the pressure. Everything seems out to slow us down — problems with skins, trees getting in our way, the deep snow. Right now I'm in the lead, plowing out tracks for the others.

I stop above an open slope. After forcing our way through endless trees it's good to come across an opening. Josh keeps talking about blue sky somewhere, but what I'm seeing is a wall of grey and ballooning white clouds in the distance. It looks like the next weather system is about to ambush us.

I wait for the others to draw up beside me. "What do you think?" I ask, staring down the slope.

Josh takes the shovel from his pack and slices it into the snow. After studying the snow profile he says, "To be honest, I'm not enthusiastic. The slope is steep and we aren't sure where it'll land us, but it may be our only chance, given the time left."

"How about Chic and me heading down a ways to check out the slope?" Roc asks.

"Good enough. It'll give me time to update our search coordinator at the lodge. Finn and I will wait for you to say the word before starting down. We don't want to overload the slope."

After giving my avalanche beacon a good-luck pat, I follow Roc down. We go easy, as Josh warned, and don't ski aggressively. Each time I turn, snow sloughs off with a sound like water slurping across sand. Not healthy. Roc and I stop for a consult. In the end he decides to call the other two down. "Some minor sloughing, but the slope held up reasonably well," he radios.

We watch as Josh heads off. Finn waits a minute or two and follows him. So far, so good. We turn our attention to what lies below us. Then, without warning a shout comes from above. "Avalanche!"

Finn has taken a header and, like some primeval beast

coming to life, the slope around him starts to stir. It slides, then slows down, until Finn suddenly pitches forward again and sets it going. The snow gathers strength and swallows him in a blur of white.

That's enough for us. Roc and I carve turns that take us into the trees. In the rush I crunch my head against a branch and tumble sideways. The cold breath of the avalanche brushes my face as it sweeps past.

"Are you two all right?" My brother slides to a stop beside us.

Roc spits snow and mumbles, "Yes," from the tree hole where he's crashed. Josh and I salvage him and we head down to find Finn.

No talk is needed. We've practised this so many times it's as automatic as breathing — avalanche transceivers are set to search mode, probes are pulled out and shovels ready. The three of us move in a line down the slope, the arrows on our transceivers guiding us. Our skis rattle across the balls of snow at the toe of the slide. We're zeroing in on Finn and his buried beacon.

"Straight ahead — something sticking out," Josh shouts. He pounces on the spot and uncovers a half-buried glove.

"You think he's down there?" I'm ready to start probing.

Josh shakes his head. "Not sure. His glove was ripped off by the force of snow. What are the numbers on your transceiver saying?"

I hold my beacon close to the snow, moving it from side to side, backwards and forwards. My eyes focus on the numbers, 0.8. Move forward, 1.1. Getting colder. Move to the right, 0.9. A bit warmer. Now left, 0.9, then 1.2. No-go in that direction. My hands are shaking. I can't hold the beacon steady.

Josh bypasses me. "You're off course on the left. I read 0.7 here. Start probing, and hurry. He's been under more than five minutes."

After fifteen minutes survival becomes iffy. A lot depends on snow conditions and whether the avalanche victim has been able to clear a breathing space around his face. I feel like such a klutz — I've wasted time with my number crunching. But I don't need Josh's automatic "hurry" response either. I'm nervous enough without it.

"I have him," Roc yells.

We grab shovels and start moving snow. Branches, chunks of bark fly out. Seconds tick by. I can't move any faster. My arms are getting tired. Then Roc's shovel grazes something.

"Oh shit, I've been shaving the poor guy's head."

Josh is clearing away snow with his hands. "Go easy, Roc. You know how he loves his hair."

"I know . . . I know." We laugh like it's one big, crazy joke and keep scraping away snow.

Within minutes we have Finn uncovered. He's okay, nothing broken. His skis came loose as they should and a pole got bent. He's one lucky dude. As slides go this was peanut-sized.

Is Finn back to normal? Hardly. After five minutes or more buried under snow, a person will be suffering from cold and shock and possibly blacked out from lack of oxygen. Finn is shaking like he has the before-exam jitters. After checking Finn over we give him a down vest and make him drink half a Thermos of tea. The tea was great for warmth, but now the poor guy has to pee. More delay.

Josh is struggling with what has happened. "Sorry, I think that I made a wrong call on that slope."

Finn has joined ranks again. "No way. If I hadn't wiped out I'm ninety-nine percent certain the slide would never have happened."

"Um . . . thanks, Finn."

For sure it's rough for the leader when things go wrong. Now it's my turn to give Josh a brotherly pat on the back. He doesn't seem to notice. I hope he still isn't peeved at me. I thought I was doing more-or-less okay.

But time marches on, as my dad likes to say. It's after three. I've been watching the clouds closing in, full of snow I guess. We've been so busy we haven't had time to check out our surroundings. From what I can see we're parked on a wide bench that drops off into a cliff.

Josh marks our position on his GPS. "It looks negotiable, at least from where we're standing."

The crew agrees on our next move — head in the general direction of the ski resort, hoping the bench is continuous and will land us somewhere below the point where I found the broken branch. Sounds complicated? You bet. Nothing on Suicide Scarp is straightforward.

Josh starts breaking trail and I take up the rear. My skis are on automatic. I'm waiting for that so-called second wind to take over and push me forward. My thoughts are mostly focused now on the coming night.

20 *a clue in red*

SUNDAY, 3:35 PM: CHIC

Roc and I are behind Finn and it's obvious he is in trouble. He's not groaning or complaining, but he's falling further and further behind Josh. He stops and leans over his skis. Roc sprints ahead to alert Josh and I stay with Finn. "Just a bit dizzy, I'll be fine in a minute," he tells me.

"We'll take a break."

I hand him a water bottle and watch him drink. When he tilts his head back I can tell his neck hurts. Knowing how he was tossed around in the avalanche, that's not surprising. He kept telling us he was okay to go on and we wanted to believe him because we're short of time and manpower and we can't leave him on his own.

"How are you doing, Finn?"

He straightens his shoulders and stretches both arms. "I'll be fine. You three carry on and I'll follow."

Josh arrives back in time to hear the last bit. "We're not all going on, Finn. You need to take a break."

"Look, I don't want to hold things up. I'm a bit tired and my neck is sore. So what? I'm up to going."

"Given the situation I have to believe you, Finn. But I want you to dump the heavy pack you are carrying. The three of us will divvy up your stuff."

Josh waves Roc and me on. "Do a quick recce. I'll radio the others to let them know what's up. Finn and I will follow slowly."

"Will do."

And we're off. It's already 4:05 and there's not much daylight left. As we push ahead, the ledge becomes narrower and begins to slope downwards. It doesn't look promising. "I think we're at a dead end," Roc says finally.

"Yeah?"

"We might as well retrace our ski tracks and meet the others. See what Josh suggests. Maybe we missed something along the way."

"How be I hang around here and try shouting again? The sound bounces all over the place, thanks to these cliffs. It'd be tough for anyone to hear us."

"Good thinking, Chic. You can always radio back if you hear anything."

A couple minutes' poling and Roc is out of sight. I stare at the cliffs, rising like an impenetrable barrier above me. It's very still. No wind, no snow drifting down for a change. Even though I know the other three are nearby, I feel cut off. I cup my hands together and shout, "Halloo ... Cass ... Luc." No answer except my own calls echoing back.

Wait a minute, I hear something else — the voice, or whatever it was, seemed to be coming from above. I call again. No sound. I want so badly to hear something. Nothing moves — no branch cracks, no snow plops down from the trees. My arms hang limp by my sides, my skis are frozen to the spot.

Finally the others crowd around me. I'm glad of the noise that breaks the silence that had me trapped. "What's going on?" Josh asks.

"I thought I heard a voice or something."

We stand there listening. Nothing. I must have been dreaming. Another zero for me. What's Josh up to anyhow? I see him swivelling around. He has one arm raised and is pointing ...

"Take a look up there, Chic."

It's the usual — a cliff plastered with snow, another ledge above that and so it goes. But there's something else up there, something red — a blotch of colour against the white. How could I have missed it?

Within seconds Josh is on the VHF radio, calling in the nearest group. "Group two, group two. SAR base command here. We're onto something. We need more manpower right away. Follow our tracks. Don't try any shortcuts. You'll see the slope leading down here that avalanched when one of my crew fell. If possible, get what snow is left up top to slide before you start down. Over."

"Roger. We're on the way. Anything else?"

"Yes, alert our support group with the sled, to stand by."

"How long do you think it'll take them?" I ask Josh.

"Three-quarters of an hour max. In the meantime we're going to find a route up this little cliff and find out who or what is there."

Josh is sounding his gung-ho self again and the mood is contagious. Even Finn, who was bent over his poles, springs to life. He stays behind with Roc while Josh and I head off in opposite directions along the ledge. This little cliff, as my brother describes the vertical rock, snow and bush overhead, looks pretty gnarly to me.

I'm backtracking and thrashing my way through trees toward the cliff base when one ski disappears down a hole. I drag it out, then my other ski sinks. Must be a gremlin making trouble down there. Finally it clicks. This sinkhole is actually a track. Snow has drifted in and camouflaged the ski or boot marks.

I need to see where this goes. Once in the path my skis stay there. I sink, drag myself up, then sink again. Sometimes I float for a whole ski length before going down. Sweat drips from my forehead and stings my eyes. I wipe it dry with one sleeve. Somebody else must have been struggling here. In spite of the twists and turns, I'm being pulled steadily toward the cliff base.

Maybe I should turn and report back. No way, I have to see where this goes. I stumble into an opening where snow lies heaped beneath the steep face. I scuff the snow with my skis. Something grabs my attention there. I bend over to look. "Blood!" I yelp and pull back. Turn and retrace my tracks. I can't go fast enough.

"Any luck?" Josh calls when he sees me coming.

Until my skis run over his skis, I don't say a word. But boy, do I start talking then. I'm like an alarm clock going off.

"Hold it, we can hardly follow you," Josh says.

And that's exactly what I can't do.

"We better all go take a look, like right now." Roc interrupts the two of us and manages to switch me off.

21 the overhang

SUNDAY, 4:15 PM: CHIC

Josh surveys the snow piled beneath the cliff. "Nothing here now, but somebody came by recently. I'd guess within the last few hours."

As usual Josh is right. I saw blood on the snow and panicked. Without taking a second look I convinced myself there was a body somewhere underneath. Josh knows I freaked out, but he doesn't rub it in. I'm grateful.

"Here's how I see it, Chic. The snow slid when some-one was climbing down. Whoever it was got hurt in the descent, then wandered off, looking for a way out. We need to check where the tracks go and also if there is anyone left up top."

I keep nodding my head. Okay, okay, I get the picture.

No point going on and on. I look at the light filtering through the trees. It's growing dimmer by the minute.

Meanwhile, Josh is on the VHF radio, contacting the lodge and the two other groups. "Where's your location, team two?"

"We made it down the steep slope. No problem. Over."

"Excellent. Another twenty minutes or so should see you here."

"Roger."

"Team one, can you hear me? We haven't located the missing skiers, but we do have tracks. We'll call if and where we need your rescue sled."

Josh is on fast-forward. He'll stay with Finn, man the radio and relay any news to headquarters down below. Roc is to follow the tracks and see where they lead. I'm to head up and check out the red marker we saw. Why me? I've heard Josh say more than once, *I've never seen anyone knuckle their way over rock like you, Chic.* He's come to believe it, I guess. Plus he wants to get me working. "You need to put all that nervous energy to some good use," he tells me.

Problem is, I'm seeing mostly snow, with some rock thrown in to make it interesting. I kick off my skis. Take the first step onto rock. It's slick with snow. The crux is staring me in the face. How to lever myself onto the next projecting rock? By clearing away snow with one boot, I gain a few centimetres. I take a step up and my boot dives into a crack. This must be where all the rubble from above has landed. Snow on near vertical scree — a tricky combo.

Josh watches me from below. There's nothing he can do to help. A rope isn't much use here — it would only dislodge loose rock, bringing down snow. And placing protection? Forget it. In loose snow, ice screws don't work. And even if I had a deadman snow anchor along, it'd be tough to bury it securely among all these rocks.

Yeah, the best thing is good old muscle power. I punch both my arms into the snow up to the elbows. Now spread-eagle my legs. Reach the left foot up and over. What I need is size thirteen boots. No go. I gotta relax this stretch before I split apart.

"Chic, can't you find a better handhold? Should I come up and help?" And so on. All he needs is a bull-horn. I know Josh is worried and wants to help, but I'd like to turn him off.

After resting for a couple minutes I repeat the operation. And this time I nail it. Both feet are onto the projecting rock. My legs are trembling from the effort — they feel like elastic bands on the loose. I shake each leg out before moving onto the snow. It's steep. My nose is practically pecking at the snow.

It's slow going. I punch out another step. The snow collapses and one foot slides back, but the lower one holds. "Are you all right?" Josh calls for about the tenth time. I haven't breath left to answer him.

I clutch the first, solitary tree and pull myself up. Some bark has been newly stripped from one side. Somebody must have come by in a hurry. Where the slope becomes less steep a mini-forest takes over. Branches whip across my face and catch me like I'm a fly stuck in a spider web. I push aside the last hemlock branch that's holding me back and find myself on a ledge. Is anyone here, anyone still here?

An awesome rock face looms above me. In places it's overhanging. I zero in on the red thing Josh spotted. I stumble toward it. Wallow in the knee deep snow and grab what turns out to be a red toque hanging from a ski pole. There are signs of tracks everywhere. One set of tracks leading from the ski pole looks more recent. I follow them towards the base of the cliff, calling as I go, "Cass! Luc!"

I keep hoping to hear a voice. I stop once to listen. Nothing except wind shaking the stunted trees — sign of the next storm moving in. I shove on. The snow is packed down near the base of the cliff, making the going easier. I imagine someone pacing back and forth, puzzling where to go next. No surprise. I glance at the rock and snow hanging above me. What a place to be trapped!

I reach for my VHF and call Josh. "I found a red ski toque. Am following tracks. They look recent. Over."

"Well done, Chic. Keep us informed."

I stumble over something buried in the snow. Jab a hand against the rock to steady myself and discover the broken ski that tripped me. I must be getting close to . . . to something. I make my way along the cliff edge. It's undercut, forming a sort of roof overhead. Did they crawl underneath to wait out the worst weather? I get down on my hands and knees and peer inside. Looks like a cave. It's difficult to see in the dim light.

As I reach my arm underneath, it touches something that isn't rock. I drag out my headlamp and aim the beam inside. *It's a hand!* I let the headlamp beam waver further up until I see a face.

"Cass!"

She is lying on her stomach, one arm stretched forward, like she's been trying to crawl out. "Cass," I repeat in a whisper. No answer. When I touch her face I feel the coldness there.

My fingers are dancing all over the place as I call Josh on the VHF. "I found her."

"How is she?"

"I don't know yet."

"No sign of Luc?"

I zoom my headlamp around the overhang to make doubly sure. "Nope."

"I'll notify the crew. They should be here any minute."

"I'll let down a handline to speed things up."

"Roger."

There's no time to rig anything high-tech. I push my way through the stunted trees to the open slope, kick out a platform there, and uncoil the rope I've been carrying on my pack. I find the sturdiest-looking tree, hitch my rope end around it, and let the other end slither down the slope. Then I give the rope a sharp tug to make sure it's firm.

I can't seem to move fast enough as I head back to Cass. Everything seems to be in overdrive except me — tree branches whipping about in the wind, storm clouds moving in, darkness snuffing out what's left of our day. I crunch my boots into the snow and lean forward. Without warning the rock and I meet head on. I rub my forehead. Uh-oh, that's the penalty for running around with my brain half shut. But trust me, Cass, I'm trying my best, my very best.

22 ordeal

SUNDAY, 6:00 PM: LUC

I don't check my watch anymore. It's too dark. I was careful at first. I followed the streambed, but stayed high, worried about the gully and possibly open water below. Very tired now. Hard to stay alert. I look for lights from the ski resort, a glow in the sky. Nothing. Shout until I'm hoarse. My voice goes lost in the trees and cliffs. Lost like me. Snowflakes hit my face. I'm running out of options.

I can't sit down — I'd never get up. But my body is whispering, *Sit down, lie down, Luc. Just for a minute. It'll be fine. No worries.* It sounds sweet. I want to listen. But I plug my ears. Have to keep going. I shove myself through the snow. Shirt is wet with sweat. Stop and it'll freeze like cardboard. Another two steps. Then rest. I lean against a small tree. Slippery with snow, it spins me off and I go crashing.

A sudden edge. Sliding and then a stop. Sound of water somewhere. Water? It's soaking my foot. I jerk the foot back. Can't walk anymore. Good leg now wonky. So I slide on my bum. Easy where there's ice underneath. But cold, very cold. The streambed walls me in. Steep banks on both sides. No way out. Only down. And my sweater feels like cardboard. Sorry, Cass, not sure I can make it.

23 *inside the cave*

SUNDAY, 5:10 PM: CHIC

I clear away snow around the overhang entrance and crawl inside the cave where Cass is lying. She doesn't move. She has to be hypothermic and not . . . I start to think the other word and stop. Further injuries? It's hard to say. What I do know is she was crawling toward the entrance and probably not that long ago. I don't want to move her. More experienced guys will be here soon; I'll let them decide when it's safe to move her. The one thing I can do is slip some insulation under her chest. *Careful there, Chic.* I focus my headlamp on her face. The whiteness of glacial ice is reflected back at me.

"Cass?"

No reply.

All the courses I've taken, all the first-aid sessions, all the things I've learned about hypothermia, churn inside my head. She must be very cold. But has it reached the critical point where her core body temperature has fallen below 31 degrees?

"Hurry — please. I need help." The chill air of the cave smothers my whisper. Except for the rustle of my jacket and my own breathing there is no sound.

I kneel down beside Cass and tuck my vest around her neck. She hasn't got a hat on. I find one lying on the ground. It's icy cold. I warm it in my hands and drape it over her head. I imagine the cold stroking her skin, then creeping inside to capture her heart, lungs, brain. I try to delete that image. Trouble is, if the cold is too far gone, it's worse than useless to pile on more clothes. It just acts like insulation holding the cold in.

"Cass?" I thought I heard a sigh. But I'm so hyper I could hear the beat of butterfly wings.

I take her hand in mine. I move my fingers over her wrist — searching for any sign of a pulse. My fingers are too clumsy. It's like the cold is contagious. Is it me shivering, or is it Cass? I'm not sure. Shivering is a good sign — these words from the first-aid manual help me to focus. *Come on Cass, shiver. Give me some sign you're still alive.* I lean my face close to hers. *Yes.* I can feel her breath on my face. It's there, in a thin stream. She's alive.

"C-Cass." I stumble over her name.

Her eyes don't open, but a whisper falls from her mouth. "Luc?" I wait to hear more. Nothing. She's as lifeless as before.

"It's me, Chic. You remember me? I've come to help."

Did I see her head move? I try again. "It's me, Chic. I want to help, but I'm new to this game. The more experienced people are coming soon." I doubt she hears me, but the one-way conversation helps to keep me on track.

I ransack my pack looking for anything useful. I grab my Thermos filled with warm apple juice, lemon, and water. She's probably badly dehydrated. But I forgot — there's no way I can move her into a sitting position. I take a long swig myself then screw the cap on again. Next thing I drag out is a couple of thermal pads. "Cass, I got something here that'll help to warm you."

She is trying to say something. I lean my face close to listen. "Luc?"

"Dammit." I'm sick of that name. "Don't you get it, Cass? Luc is the guy who got you into this fix. He went off and left you." A second later I'm kicking myself. What if she is aware and heard my whisper? I'm trying to help, not make her upset.

While I open the two thermal packs and stuff them inside an extra pair of heavy socks, I keep up the monologue. "Listen Cass, I'm putting one thermal pack on your back, the other on the arm closest to me."

As I reach under the sleeve of her jacket I feel warmth there. I don't understand. Her face, everywhere else is cold. She moans softly. I must have moved her arm. And it obviously hurts. I pull down the sleeve as gently as I can.

When is the crew coming? They're taking forever. Treating hypothermia is a complicated business — go take a look at the volumes written about it. I think I've been doing all right, but I'd like some backup. The hat has slipped off Cass's head. I push it back and rest my arm across her shoulders. "At least I hope I'm doing okay, Cass."

So here we are, Cass and me, sitting side by side. It'd be great if she wasn't comatose and I wasn't worried out of my mind. What's keeping everyone? I uproot myself from Cass's side and look outside. No one in sight, but I hear voices from below. I want to chew them out: *Don't you guys realize that she could die?*

I want to chew Luc out too. *You made some bad mistakes, dude. It's almost always smarter to stay put. Chances of being found are better then. You ought to have known that, given your mountain experience.* Then I think, oh sure, it's easy for me to play the expert now. But what would I have done in the same circumstances? Lost in gnarly terrain, a buddy injured, no chance of a helicopter rescue because of bad weather, the thought of another night out . . .

When I set out this morning I had first-aid courses, avalanche workshops, practice sessions, all the book stuff neatly filed away inside my head. "And you know what, Cass? I can even spell your name in classic radio operator mode. You don't hear this anymore. So listen in, okay? 'Charlie, Alpha, Sierra, Sierra, means CASS. You read me?'"

But the truth is, I've landed in a real life situation and it's way different from the book stuff. I keep asking myself if I've followed proper search and rescue protocol, as Josh calls it. Actually, I haven't done much but sit here, hold her hand and blame the others for being slow. What should I have done? I start going over my checklist again. Check for pulse, signs of breathing, place insulation where possible . . . Around I go.

24 paramedic

SUNDAY, 5:40 PM: CHIC

I hear voices and boots crunching across the snow. Finally
— it'll be Josh and the other crew. I can still hear his
words when I radioed that I had found Cass. *Good going,
Chic.* Will he still say this after talking to me now? If and
when I know Cass is out of danger, then I'll be patting
myself on the back and saying "Good going, Chic."

Josh appears at the overhang entrance. "Chic, I want
you to give our paramedic here a quick rundown on the
patient's condition — anything you know or don't know.
Then get out of the picture, pronto. Understand?"

I see the paramedic bending down at the overhang
entrance and looking in. He's tall and having problems
with the head room. I lend him a hand to speed things

up. After switching on his headlamp he looks around and whistles softly. "You could be buried alive here and nobody would ever know."

He takes off the hat half hiding his face and now I'm the one doing the whistling, at least in my head. Our paramedic is a woman. Guess I shouldn't be surprised, seeing as more women are going into search and rescue.

We talk quietly, so the patient won't hear. "So what's your observation?"

"Severe hypothermia." Like Josh said, I keep it short.

"What you'd expect, and — ?"

"She's conscious, but not responding. Doesn't appear to be shivering."

"What action have you taken, if any?"

"I slipped some insulation underneath her and placed one thermal pad on her shoulder area, another on her arm. I only had two."

"They weren't essential. And you didn't move her?"

"Of course not, it'd be risky not knowing . . ."

"Good. Go on."

"Uh, one arm is probably broken. I wasn't able to examine it properly. The skin was warm to touch and —"

"Which one?"

"The left."

"Did you observe anything else?"

"Not really." I feel like a sidekick, kneeling here and mumbling on while this super-efficient lady grills me.

"We need to evacuate her ASAP. As soon as I've checked her over and stabilized the arm, I'll need help moving her out. Without a heli-lift, it will be difficult and, believe me, time is of the essence when we're dealing with hypothermia. Now head out, all right? I haven't got much room to work here."

As I crawl out I feel as if I'm deserting Cass. It gives me some idea of how Luc must have felt when he left her behind. "You're in good hands," I whisper back.

Compared to the reflected light inside the cave, the outside world is dark. The new moon that was shedding some light on the scene before is holed up behind clouds. Snowflakes that I can't see melt as they touch my face. Headlamps trace thin lines through the night and gradually, as my eyes adjust to the change, five figures appear.

Josh is talking. "Our second team has brought the emergency stretcher. It's ready and waiting below. They've been rigging up the rescue harness- and pulley-system. We've been stomping the snow down, so it'll be easier to move our patient. I told Finn to stay below and watch for Roc. We don't know whether he's had any luck following the tracks."

"You haven't asked me how Cass is," I say, when Josh has finished his spiel.

"I was leaving that to our paramedic."

"You might have asked me, seeing as I was in there with her."

"I realize that."

"Oh, forget it."

We're both on edge. We try to give each other some leeway.

"I should have asked you, Chic. In the rush I sometimes forget things, okay?"

"Yeah, I understand."

"I'd like you to head down and check with Finn and Roc. Give them the thumbs-up and say we're coming."

It's a relief to be off and following instructions. I'm no longer in a cramped cave, feeling useless. Though I felt bad being thrown out, I know there's a first-aid professional looking after Cass.

I run along the now well-worn trail to where the rescue ropes are suspended. Down below, I can see Finn and Roc's headlamps spinning in a bizarre dance. I take one rope, thread it through a figure eight and rappel down the steep pitch. A couple of foot bounces over snow-covered rocks is all it takes.

The two headlamps float toward me. "How is she?"

"Alive, but that's about all I can say. The paramedic is with her. They'll be lowering her in a few minutes."

"Wish I could say the same for Luc," Roc says.

In the light shed by his headlight, I can see that he looks glum. "So?"

"I followed his tracks for as long as I thought it was safe. The guy was having one epic struggle. His tracks disappeared into a stream gully."

We're interrupted by sounds from above, as the crew prepares to lower Cass in the rescue harness. Josh is taking her down. And I know she couldn't be in better hands. All systems a go, as he likes to say.

25 *on the way*

SUNDAY, 6:20 PM: CHIC

I'm focused on the scene above us — the sound of voices, the flash of headlamps. The crew has managed to move Cass from the overhang and onto the rescue stretcher. They must be struggling in the darkness with the restraining straps. I can see the headlamps zeroing in on one spot. How's she doing, I wonder, with all the moving? I wish I was there, helping. As the rescue sling swings closer I can see that Josh is with her. It's finally touchdown and I'm waiting to steady the harness and help Josh.

As we prepare to lower Cass onto the waiting stretcher, her eyes suddenly flick open. She sees me first because I'm bending over her. Doesn't say anything, just stares for a second, then closes her eyes. Did she recognize the ugly mug behind my headlamp?

"You know her?" One of the guys asks.

"Um . . . yes."

"Well, she seemed fixated on you, all right."

I'm struggling to tighten the straps holding her legs and chest — just that one blink of her eyes has thrown me off balance. Josh huffs and puffs, and then gently elbows me to one side to take over. The stretcher here is his newest high-tech baby. It's all plastic, folds around the patient when she's placed inside, glides nicely over snow, and weighs only eight kilograms. Every search and rescue group should have one, Josh says. Incidentally, they're not cheap.

"Chic . . ." My name comes in a whisper. The sound instantly switches my attention away from Josh's technological marvel.

"Chic." I see Cass's lips moving. With my heart pounding like I'm in a downhill ski race, all I can do is mumble, "Uh, yes?"

"Luc?"

Josh waves a warning finger when he sees me making a face. "Don't add worry," he whispers.

I don't want to talk, I don't want to think about Luc right now, anyhow. Having Cass beside me shuts down any other thoughts. When the plastic sides of the stretcher are partially folded over her body, it looks too much like a coffin. With her closed eyes and pale face she seems far away from the chaos around her. Everyone is hurrying, but what if it's already too late for Cass? I tuck in a blanket that's come loose. I have to do *something*. I don't breathe easy until Josh gives us our marching orders.

And what about Luc? I seem to have added him to my worry list. I can't help feeling sorry for him. We're leaving the mountain without finding him. Roc reached a dead end where the tracks disappeared into a stream gully. "It's too risky expanding the search in darkness and with another storm pushing in," Josh has told us.

He's right. None of us feel good leaving the job half done, but our first concern now is Cass. I hear Josh putting in a call to the ambulance. It has to be ready and waiting when we reach the ski lodge.

At first the going is easy. Three guys up front grip the towing harness and two behind keep the sled steady as we make our way along the ledge. There are four web handles on each side of the sled and I'm manning one of them. If we half lift the sled over rough spots it makes for a smoother, faster ride. Josh is moving us right along. He wants to be up the steep slope before more snow increases the avalanche danger.

With our headlights bobbing every which way we

must look like a ship lost in a stormy sea. And it's how I feel with the snow sluicing down and shrinking our world to a metre or so on each side. Talk about tough going — we manoeuvre the sled around trees and over bumps and snow-blown drifts, all the while trying to keep it steady. I sing to myself, tell myself how tough I am, anything to keep going.

Josh's voice crash-lands into my inner world. "We'll take a short break at the bottom of the steep slope here. If you have a problem with loose skins or wonky gear, now is the time to fix anything. It'll be grunt work getting the sled over the avalanche debris."

Grunt work is an understatement. We have to keep lifting the sled over frozen chunks of snow. Even with skins I can't get decent traction. Once past the avalanche debris the slope steepens and we're forced into a diagonal track, which means the sled keeps slipping sideways. Two of us go ahead trying to punch out a track. It helps, but we're all bushed by the time we reach the top. Group one is waiting there with the standard rescue sled which has a proper pulling bar. It'll make the going way easier.

"Quick stop while we transfer our patient," Josh says.

Then he's on the phone again, talking to our man at the lodge. "You're still getting phone calls from him?" I hear Josh saying. He turns to me after he has signed off.

"It seems that Luc's father is making a real nuisance of himself. He's continually phoning the lodge, saying why don't we do this, why don't we do that. I suppose it's his way of showing some concern for his son. He says he would come up himself, but both he and his wife are in New York or someplace."

"You have to feel sorry for anyone with an old man like that. Count ourselves lucky, eh Josh?"

He drops me a big-brother smile, something I'd been missing. "We don't have an absentee dad, that's for sure. You have to love the opposite, don't you, Chic?"

For a few seconds we meet as brother to brother again. But my smile gets scrapped when I hear the paramedic talking quietly to Josh. "We have to get this girl to hospital. She's fading fast. It's difficult to get a pulse."

"We have her transferred and strapped in," one of the crew tells Josh.

"Then let's roll."

Although it's snowing heavily, our ski tracks from earlier in the day are still visible. We make good time pulling the heavier sled. As we near the ski resort boundary and the first groomed run I can feel the energy level rising. Our poles churn the snow, our breath spirals into the night sky. We're near the end.

26 end of the road

SUNDAY, 6:45 PM: LUC

I hear water falling. Underneath? Somewhere. I slide faster. Spin off my bum and onto my side. Try to brake. But there is nothing to hold on to. It's all ice and water running fast and I'm falling with it. Hitting a rock and slipping on ice. And then quiet — for a long time.

I open my eyes. Shut them. Open them again. At least something works. I try to move. No go. Finally stop trying. Don't know what hurts. Everything sore. I open my mouth: "Help." But I'm drowned out by that water sound.

Did I call out? Doesn't matter. It's too late. Nobody will hear me. I won't last the night. Too cold and wet. Yes, it does matter. Have to keep calling, long as I can. Long as my mouth opens. All I can do now. "Help." Wind and snow and water trap my sound. "Help."

27 toru's turn

SUNDAY, 7:40 PM: CHIC

The *Out of Bounds* sign marking the edge of the patrolled area is close. I can't see it, but I can hear the creaking of the wooden board as it sways back and forth in the wind. We slide the rescue sled past the rope and our skis hit the packed run. Big relief — we're almost there. I keep thinking of Luc, somewhere on Suicide Scarp. It's dark and dumping snow. He has to be feeling desperate.

"We need someone else to help brake the sled. Roc?" Josh waves him to the back. Guiding a rescue sled down a groomed run with someone inside is tough work. It's not for muscle-challenged wimps, that's for sure.

I'm more than happy when Josh tells me to head

down and talk with the ambulance attendants. "See you in a few minutes," I whisper to Cass as I ski past her.

Far below me I can make out the lights of the ski resort and the runs that are open for night skiing. In the falling snow the lights waver and look like stars flickering in a night sky. I point my skis downhill. Which is more unreal — the world I left behind or the one I'm heading toward? My headlamp skips across the moguls, showing me the way. Cass isn't far behind. Let's hope the world she is heading into stays good.

I stop by the lodge and kick off my skis, then head towards the ambulance waiting in the parking lot. Josh has already radioed the paramedic, but I give them an update. "Ten minutes and they should be here," I tell the driver.

I hear the ambulance attendant contacting the hospital. "Patient with severe hypothermia, broken arm, possibly other complications. ETA forty-five minutes to an hour, depending on traffic."

I head into the lodge like Josh told me to do, looking for Cass's parents. There are a pile of people milling around, everyone hungry for news — including some reporters. Like vultures around a kill, I think. I finally spot Cass's folks. They are sitting on a bench by the window, arms around each other. They haven't noticed me yet;

their focus is on the window. I want to turn away while there's still time. I don't know what to say. But I have to let them know what's up. Josh said it was crucial.

Cass's dad, maybe seeing my reflection in the glass, turns around. "How is she? Have they arrived yet?"

"They'll be here any minute. She's hypothermic, like you'd expect. One of you may want to ride down with her in the ambulance. We should head out."

The rescue sled pulls up as we get to the ambulance. The crowd around Cass gives way as her parents hurry up. Me? I don't get a chance for another look. Cass is bundled into the ambulance, her mom follows her inside, and that's it. The ambulance speeds away, sirens sounding. Talk about an abrupt ending. I feel like someone has hit me on the head and I'm stumbling around with a concussion.

The whole crew drifts about, looking dazed. The adrenaline that's been keeping us going is fading. "You guys need some rest and something to eat while we decide what's next. Let's go inside," Josh says.

But it's a zoo inside with all the reporters and sensation-seekers crowding the lodge. All eyes are on Josh. Someone from the *Times Reporter* shoves a mike in his face and asks a dozen questions at the same time.

Somehow Josh handles it like a pro and after five minutes or so of flashing cameras, he manages to tear himself loose from the pack. "My volunteers are tired. They need to eat. No more questions," he tells the one reporter who won't call it quits.

I'm standing beside Josh when I notice our old man hurrying towards us. Mom is with him and they're actually holding hands. Even from a distance I can see his face is screwed up. I've never seen him look so old and tired. Worried, for sure, but what else is there? We'll find out in a minute.

It starts before he even reaches us. "Your mother and I have been worrying all day, looking out at the weather and knowing what it must be like on the mountain. You didn't communicate with us, which added to our worry. Where exactly you were, how the search was progressing . . . we knew virtually nothing. A blank slate — we suspected the worst."

I'm blinking my eyes open and shut in alarm mode when suddenly I feel a pair of arms around me. *What?* It's dad hugging me and mom has her arms around Josh.

"We are so glad you're safe," they are saying.

"And to think that you were able to navigate in such treacherous terrain, under the worst possible weather conditions, and find at least one of the skiers. And on your first mission, Chic. I guess I'm resigned to the fact that you are both mountain men, no matter what I say or think. The mountain world is alluring all right, both beautiful and deadly. Who should know this better than me? Well . . . we are very proud of you both," Dad finishes his spiel.

I swallow hard and blink a big one. "You are?"

"Most certainly. Only, next time, you might consider being a bit more communicative." I detect the start of his familiar upside-down smile — a good sign.

Josh excuses himself to join the rest of his crew in the restaurant. I say goodbye to my folks. "Not sure when we'll be home, but will let you know as soon as possible."

"You do that." My dad has the trace of a real smile on his face.

I'm heading toward the restaurant to join the others when Toru comes hurrying up. Where was he all this time? I never noticed him in the crowd.

"Sit down for a minute. I need to talk with you," he says, pushing me onto the nearest sofa.

This is not like Toru. "What's up?"

Toru sits down beside me. "It's about Luc. Nobody is talking about him, nothing is happening, and he's still lost out there."

"Listen, Toru, the SAR guys haven't given up on Luc. They're just taking a quick break and having a bite to eat. And I'd like to join them. We've been going since early this morning, remember?"

"I know you're all tired and hungry. But I can't just wait here doing nothing. What if every minute is crucial? I could have done more to stop him from going out of bounds. I should have tried, instead of shrugging my shoulders and saying goodbye. I'm his friend and friends try to help one another. Right now I'm feeling like a failure — a no-good friend. Don't you understand, Chic?"

"So what can I do? Or, more to the point, what do *you* want to do, Toru?"

"I want to head out and look for Luc."

"By yourself and in this weather? Be serious."

"I'm dead serious and I'll tell you why. I know the terrain around here as well as anybody. And I know Luc possibly better than anyone else does. Guaranteed, he will be fighting his way down the mountain if he's still alive. He has the strength of a tiger when the odds are against him."

"You know he could be anywhere, Toru."

"Of course, he could be anywhere. But if he is following one of the many stream gullies he'd likely come out somewhere close to the Far Easterly cross-country run. I want to check it out."

He has a point. But what would Josh say to this? "Where's Nick? Can you get him to go with you?"

Toru waves toward a figure hunched over a table in the far corner. "He won't budge. He said it's none of my business, that it's up to search and rescue and I should quit meddling."

Josh waves to me from the restaurant. "You coming, Chic? We're ordering some food and planning our next move."

"I'm coming in a minute. Go ahead."

Toru grabs my arm. "Will you come with me? Wait around and it could be too late for Luc."

"I'm hearing what you're saying, Toru, but I can't just take off. Imagine how that would fly with Josh. I'm sort of on probation with search and rescue."

"Then I'm going now. It's not as if I'm skiing out of bounds. I'll be following the cross-country run."

"Yeah, I know how that goes. You don't find Luc near there and you just keep going."

A weak smile and a shoulder shrug and he's off. "See you then, Chic."

"Hold it," I call after him. "I'll talk to Josh. If he gives me the green light I'll follow you and try to catch up."

He waves back, but I can't hear what he is saying. I turn and head into the restaurant where Josh and the bunch are sitting around one big table. Their food has just arrived. I'm mega-tempted but I head straight to

Josh and whisper in his ear exactly what Toru is up to. "What do you think, should I follow him?"

A long pause as he swallows a mouthful. "I think that might be wise."

I'm kind of shocked. "You really think so?"

"Yes, and I'll tell you why. From what you're telling me this is out of character for Toru. Could be he'll do something rash and get in trouble. We don't need another lost body, do we? When we're finished here, Roc and Finn and myself and one or two others will follow with the rescue sled. Though I have to admit I'm not hopeful."

"Okay, I'm off then."

"Pick up a sandwich at the snack bar. I don't want one of my team dropping from hunger."

"Will do."

"And keep to the cross-country run. It's wicked weather out there."

"For sure."

"We shouldn't be more than half an hour behind you."

"Good." And I'm out the door, all set to trample on the back of Toru's skis.

28 toru and chic

SUNDAY, 8:30 PM: CHIC

It's no surprise that the wind-whipped snow hits my face as soon as I'm on the cross-country run. It's called the Far Easterly for a good reason — it's open to all the big storms that push in from the east. I've got plenty of time to think about Luc and why I'm out looking for him. I'm more sorry for him than angry, now. If he is still alive, I wonder what's keeping him going? Thinking about Cass for one thing, same as me. Kind of weird how this puts us both in the same space.

The temperature has warmed up with the weather system that has moved in. The snow feels like a miserable combo of hail and sleet. I bend my head so the stuff doesn't hit my face straight on. Although the first loop of the Far Easterly is lit for night skiing, I don't meet a single person. Probably Toru and I are the only ones out here and I haven't caught sight of him yet.

It's not likely that Luc would have found his way to the first loop, but I still call out his name every few minutes. No luck. Where the first loop swings back toward the lodge I stop. Beyond is darkness. Should I keep going? I switch on my headlamp and shine it onto the groomed track, which is still clearly visible in spite of the blowing snow. Further ahead the beam catches only the streak of falling snow.

Hold it . . . I see a light flashing back. I hear a faint shout. It has to be Toru. My question is answered. I push ahead into the darkness, following the beam of my headlamp until I'm standing beside Toru, who is waiting for me.

"Thanks, Chic. Are you ready to plow on?"

"Half a ham sandwich and I'll be good to go."

Toru shakes his head when I hold out the other half. And we're off, skiing side by side so our headlamps better illuminate the tracks ahead. Every few minutes we shout over the wind, "Luc! Luc!" We hear nothing back.

When we reach the point where the second loop turns and heads back toward the lodge, we stop. What now? There are no set tracks to follow. We can't see more than two metres ahead. It's blizzard conditions — worse than yesterday, if that's possible.

"What do you say, Chic?"

"Josh will be here soon. Why not wait and carry on together? He said that we should stick to the cross-country run."

"Fine. You stay here and I'll keep going."

"You should wait, Toru." I don't want to be reporting back to Josh that someone else has gone missing.

"Like I told you, Chic, time matters. And if Luc did go lost beyond the opening, somewhere ahead is where he'd end up if he actually managed to work his way down."

"Sounds like a lot of 'ifs' to me."

"Well my 'ifs' are pretty carefully thought out. You know my reputation, right?" Toru gives a half laugh.

"Okay. Carry on, Toru, but don't go far. I'll wait and follow with Josh."

At the last second I remember the whistle hanging around my neck and hand it over to Toru. The sound will carry better than any voice. Two minutes later Toru's headlamp is swallowed up by the white snow in the dark night.

I'm alone and I don't like it. The scrap of confidence I felt on leaving the lodge is petering out. Every minute or so I check my watch. No sign of Josh and no word from Toru. This is insane. We're not going to find Luc in the middle of a blizzard. I have half a mind to turn and meet up with Josh when I see Toru's headlamp bouncing back toward me. He's blowing the whistle like he's an engineer sitting on a runaway train.

"I heard him! I heard Luc! His voice was coming from above. He can't be far." And Toru stops beside me, his skis grating across mine.

I try to untangle our skis and make him talk sense. "Did you mark the spot where you first heard him, Toru?"

"Yes, I left my pack there. It's not more than five minutes from here. His voice sounded very weak. If we go back and find him even hearing a friend's voice might help him to hang in there. What should we do, Chic?"

"One of us has got to stay here until Josh and the others arrive. Maybe I should go ahead because I have skins for my skis. I'll be faster climbing. Okay with you, Toru?"

"I'd like to go myself, but . . . you're right, whatever is faster. You'll see my pack where I stamped the snow down. Good luck, Chic."

There's a true friend for you. *You're lucky to be skiing with guys like him, Luc.* I turn and direct my headlamp onto Toru's ski tracks. Already the snow is sifting into them, but they are easy to follow. I'm confident that we're doing the right thing. I hope Josh will agree. He can't be far behind now.

The terrain beyond the last cross-country loop is flat and mostly bush-free, which makes for easy going. In summer it's marshy and full of animal tracks, not to mention the blackflies and mosquitoes. Winter is definitely more friendly here, just not tonight. When I reach Toru's pack I stop and drag out my skins. Because they're still wet from the last time I used them it's a struggle to get them on, and in the rush my fingers feel clumsy.

After I have them on I straighten up and look around. Above the flat ground where I'm standing, dense bush takes over. And Luc is somewhere up there. I call his name and wait for his voice: nothing, except the wind whipping tree branches back and forth. "Luc!" I call again. This time I hear a faint reply from above and slightly ahead of where I am.

Once I've oriented myself to the source of the sound, I take off. I'm into trees and making my way along what seems to be a stream gully. Every few minutes I call, "Luc!" I don't hear an answer, but I keep going in what seems to be the right direction.

I'm out of breath from climbing and shouting. My headlamp traces a narrow path between walls of darkness. I swing my head from side to side, trying to figure out what I'm getting myself into. The gully looks steeper ahead, the sides pressed closer together. It could be where the stream, mostly buried under ice and snow, catapults over rock. I'll have to exit. I'm searching for a way up and out when a voice calls from below me, "Help."

"Luc?" Because of the skins on my skis I slide clumsily backward and almost run over his body, half covered with snow. I brush some away and direct my headlight onto his face. I turn away. One look is enough. I see the pain scratched there.

Somehow his lips move. "Cass?"

"We found her. The ambulance is taking her to hospital. She'll be okay."

The only sound I hear is crying, Luc crying. I take off my jacket and drape it over his chest and neck. "Can you hear me, Luc? It's me — Chic. There's help coming in a few minutes. We'll get you out of this mess. Hang in there, buddy."

"Couldn't have lasted any . . ." Luc doesn't finish the sentence. The words come slowly, scratchy-sounding like they're coming from a deep place of pain. It's hard to hear. After that he just moans.

Gently, I brush the snow off his head and place my ski toque there. Not that it really helps. It's more to let him know that someone is close. Once when my headlamp flickers across his face I see his eyes staring blankly up at me. *Please, Luc, please, don't go and die on me.*

Other than being here, I can't do much to help Luc while I wait for Josh. I stomp the snow down to make the rescue sled transfer easier. My mind is stomping around even faster than my feet. I feel differently toward Luc now. I'm responsible for him. I want so badly to see him out of here and somehow, maybe miraculously, recovering. Was I angry at him a long time ago? Sure, but not anymore. He made some bad choices. Anyone can make mistakes. But as my dad says, you make mistakes in the mountains at your own peril.

Luc doesn't move. His mouth is open, but there is no sound coming. It's very quiet, too quiet. The trees overhead dull the sound of any wind. Below Luc and me is the frozen stream and a slow *drip, drip*, deep down where something still runs. At last I hear sounds from the outside world. It's Josh and the others coming to help.

29 end or beginning

SUNDAY, 9:45 PM: CHIC

"How is it down there?" Josh calls. Of course he's unhappy about the steep-sided stream gully, but rescue operations never take place in handy places.

"There's room for the sled. I stomped out a platform best as I could in the tight space."

As soon as our paramedic hears this, she sideslips down the bank, throws off her skis and gets to work. With blizzard conditions and now falling temperatures, speed is what counts. "Calm, cool and collected," Toru whispers as we watch her. I know exactly what he means.

After she has stabilized Luc, four of us shift him onto the sled. No sound comes from him. When my headlamp darts across his face I see no signs of life.

Josh tightens the last strap on the rescue sled. "All right, let's mush out of here. We'll follow the stream bed. It's wide enough for the sled. I suspect there will be an easier exit below where the slope eases off."

As usual, Josh is right. We half lift, half pull the sled from the gully and we're soon onto the flats. With Josh and Toru and the crew all doing their bit, it's clear sailing. Wish I could say the same for Luc, but I hope for the best. Bad luck or bad choices, it could be any one of us lying there on the stretcher.

I hear Josh behind me breathing hard and hacking and coughing. When he's stressed out and tired he can get these asthma attacks. It's been a long and rough day for him. I slow down to let him catch up. We carry on side by side, neither of us speaking, but the silence feels right. My own chest heaves with each breath. It's like I'm pulling the whole sky into my lungs — oxygen, stars, whatever else is up there. Never have I travelled so far and so fast. And I don't mean my feet — it's my thoughts, everything.

For me, the last twenty-four hours have been amazing. "Amazing." I repeat the word out loud. I know this sounds harsh — after all, two people are critically injured. But we did find them. And I've been a part of it, working alongside a bunch of experts who love what they do.

We've been together on the job for over twenty-four hours. If you ask me, I've crammed in enough to fill a whole lifetime.

When we reach the lodge Luc is immediately transferred to a waiting ambulance. I listen to the long wail as it winds its way down the hill toward town. I turn to Josh. "Pretty sad that there are no parents to ride with him."

"Rumour has it that they're finally on their way home. I hope they haven't left it too late," Josh says.

What surprises me most is to discover that Nick followed the SAR group. He never said a word the whole time, which is practically unheard-of for Nick. "I couldn't just sit around doing my usual nothing," he tells me a bit sheepishly.

By ten-thirty, the ski lodge is nearly empty. Roc, Finn, and the rest of the team have hitched a ride to town in the paramedic's van. Toru wanted to hang out with me, but his parents arrived and dragged him off to safety. With a little persuasion from Josh they agreed to give Nick a lift.

I'm finishing up the food I ordered before the restaurant shut: a double cheeseburger with a side of dill pickles and salad, and blueberry pie. Now all I need is some sleep. No chance of that until Josh has finished talking with the ski patrol and wrapped things up for the night. I'm about to curl up on a comfy chair when Josh comes over and says we can head home.

"I just spoke with the hospital. Your girlfriend seems to be recovering."

"My girlfr— you mean Cass?"

"It looks like she'll be in the hospital for a few days. She's on intravenous antibiotics to minimize the danger of any infection from her broken arm."

"And Luc?"

"No news yet. They just took him into Emergency. The paramedic was not sounding optimistic."

Josh and I pile into his van. It's cold and damp and feels very empty and quiet without the rest of the crew. It's the first time Josh and I have been alone for ages. I hear him clearing his throat once we're on the way and I keep quiet so he can have the first word.

"It's been a long day, Chic, and we're both tired."

Oh my gosh, it sounds like he's going to give me a lecture.

"You know, search and rescue is a dicey business. It's a fine balance between caution and risk-taking. As you've heard me say often enough, the leader has to err on the side of caution."

Pretty official-sounding — and yes, I've heard that one at least five times in the last twenty-four hours alone.

I'm waiting for something else, I'm not sure what exactly. When it does come it's non-stop.

"Well, Chic, you did stray close to the risk-taking edge on one or two occasions. I'm thinking especially of that moment when you discovered the broken branch above the cliff overhang and didn't answer my call. But that small clue led us to Cass. You used your head, which is more than I can say for some dudes who ski out of bounds and think they're safe as long as they can see the ski hills. By the way that's why we SAR types call the area close to runs 'slack country'."

"Good description," I mumble. My alarm system has calmed down and now I'm feeling sleepy.

"What I do know for sure, Chic, it was great having you along. In another year or so, if you want, you can be an official member of the team."

I pop awake. If I want! Now comes the real, down-to-earth, brotherly pat on the back that I've been waiting for. "Thanks, but better keep your hands on the wheel, bro," I say.

"Good advice, Chic."

"You know Mom and Dad will be jumping up and down to hear the whole story. What'll we tell them?"

"Everything, Chic, absolutely everything, even if it takes all night."

"Right on, Josh."

I settle back on the car seat and close my eyes. Tomorrow I'll visit Cass in the hospital and maybe this time around she'll know who I am. Not Luc, but Chic, the guy who rescued her. Trouble is, I'll be the speechless one. I'll have to rehearse something ahead of time.

And Luc? It's a faint hope, but I'd like to have the chance to visit him too. All I can do is keep my fingers crossed.

acknowledgements

Thanks to Markus Kellerhals, Tanya Binette, Erika Kellerhals and Robyn Budd for reading the manuscript, or sections of it, and making some very useful suggestions. Also to editor Carrie Gleason, who with her unfailing GPS pointed me in the right direction. Special thanks to Bill Phipps, avalanche forecaster for Mt. Washington ski resort who has considerable experience with Search and Rescue, for working his way through the manuscript and sharing his technical expertise. And last, but far from least, my partner Rolf Kellerhals for sharing alongside me — snow storms, whiteouts and moments of sunshine and powder snow.